About the author

In Sue Hampton's eighth novel for Pegasus, you will find her love of flowers, peace and justice, music and history. It is also a tribute to Paul, the father she loves as much as ever, who was once, long ago, a young and very brave conscientious objector.

By the same author

Spirit And Fire (Nightingale Books) 2007
ISBN 9781903491584

Shutdown (Nightingale Books) 2007
ISBN 9781903491591

Voice Of The Aspen (Nightingale Books) 2007
ISBN 9781903491607

Just For One Day (Pegasus) 2008
ISBN 9781903490372

The Lincoln Imp (Pegasus) 2009
ISBN 9781903490389

The Waterhouse Girl (Pegasus) 2009
ISBN 9781903490426

Twinside Out (Pegasus) 2010
ISBN 9781903490457

The Snowgran And Ongalonging (Pegasus) Under Production
ISBN 9781903490471

Traces

Sue Hampton

Traces

Pegasus

Chapter One

Perhaps they were always there, the ghosts. Poppy had no way of knowing. Memories, leftovers, fragments. But very few facts, and until her fourteenth summer, not much imagination either. For a long time, like all young children whose lives seemed quite normal, Poppy made a lot of assumptions. The sun would rise next morning. The water in her shower would be too hot or too cold. And everything in her world, regardless of terrible things that went on outside it, would be more or less all right. Because she assumed that world of hers had always been all right, even before she was born into it.

She was ignoring the questions because she'd forgotten she couldn't answer them, in the same way that she forgot to ask why the grass was green and water had no colour at all. But then when she was eight, a question mark that had been hanging invisibly blackened up on paper. Her new topic at school was the Victorians, and her homework was to find out about her family tree. The teacher hoped that someone would be able to trace back as far as the nineteenth century. And that was when the first clue appeared from nowhere. But it was not so much a clue as a fuzzy sort of space where the truth should have been.

Poppy had always known she only had one set of grandparents, from her American mum, Anna Beth, but because they lived in California Poppy only saw them once every couple of years. So she was used to a life without grannies, nans, gramps or pops in it, and she had more than enough brothers (three) to fill anyone's world, sometimes to bursting point. Because of all her American cousins, it took ages to work her way back to the generation before hers.

"But who was Daddy's mum?" she asked, her pencil pointing to the space on the tree above his name. David Golding looked very lonely, with no brothers or sisters alongside him and no parents above him.

No one answered at first so Poppy repeated the question, in a louder and more irresistible voice.

Her brother Nick, who was fourteen then, was staring at the computer screen as usual. It was how he did most of his studying, sometimes with moving images and music that didn't seem like work to Poppy. At last he looked up.

"Hasn't got one," he said.

Poppy knew that couldn't be right. Everybody had one, to begin with anyway.

"Has she died?"

"I suppose," said Nick, after rather a long pause and without looking away from the screen.

"No," said Ed, who was eleven, and drawing a football stadium even though Poppy didn't believe that was homework either. "Don't think so."

"Why?" asked Poppy.

"Children stop asking *why* all the time when they're about three or four," said Nick.

"Not eight," said Ed.

14

The two of them exchanged looks that weren't quite grins or laughs but meant the same thing. Poppy knew it was some kind of joke at her expense, even though she couldn't help being younger than them.

"See?" said Nick. "Even Tim's not asking why all the time."

Tim was five and building something from another planet.

"What?" he said, looking up, and when Nick and Ed exchanged looks again he repeated it, eyebrows up: "WHAT?"

But whatever the question, there were no answers on offer.

Poppy didn't give up, not at first. But when she asked her mother, she just said Dad didn't have a mum any more.

"Just a lovely auntie who brought him up ..."

"Lanky?"

"Yes, your Great Auntie Lanky."

Poppy liked her great aunt and the donkeys she looked after at the sanctuary. For a while, when she was very small, she'd thought this must be her gran, but a young, tough one.

"Did my real grandma die?"

When Poppy heard the question, it sounded different that time. It sounded bigger and shakier. Her mum looked away and stirred the pan busily. For a few moments the only sound was the crisping of the stir-fry and the fan above it.

"It's a long story, darling," she said, "and not a very happy one for Daddy."

Poppy knew what that meant. It meant it was a story nobody was going to tell her. When she explained about her homework, Mum said she'd fill in that bit for her later.

She didn't forget. Poppy saw her creep into the bedroom and slip the family tree into her book bag. She pretended to be asleep, but when Mum had gone she unfolded it and fetched her torch to see what she had written in the space.

Before Lanky, who was really Amelanchier Golding, there was a boy called Joe who only lived to be four. And then there was Sorrel. Sorrel Golding, David's mum and Poppy's grandmother.

Beside Sorrel's name, Anna Beth had written a b. for born, and a date with a question mark: 1945? She hadn't put a d. for died, or another date after it.

Poppy was in the top group for Maths. It was one of the reasons Nick and Ed called her Mini Boff. It was 2003 so the backwards calculation was easy. Her grandmother Sorrel was only fifty-eight, not nearly old enough to be dead.

Poppy hadn't quite finished with her Maths brain. Her dad, David Golding, had 1963 beside his name. So when he was born, Sorrel was only eighteen. She was a teenage mum.

And there was another question, because there was still a space. There was no m. for married beside Sorrel's name, as if Dad had no dad at all.

Three years later, when Tim had the same homework, it was Poppy's job to help him.

"Don't ask Dad who his mum was," she said. "He doesn't like to talk about her."

"Why?" he asked. "Who was his mum?"

"It's a mystery," said Poppy.

Of course that was a mistake because at that time Tim would only read books with mysteries to be solved, preferably with a sword or laser gun. He started trying to make up titles like The Mystery of the Missing Gran, and Nick and Ed joined in.

"How do you solve the mystery of the missing gran?" asked Nick. "Follow the trail of wool."

"Or the grey hairs," said Ed.

Nick scowled suddenly. "What about the mystery of the invisible dad?"

Ed screwed up his face like a mole in the spotlight.

"Who's Dad?"

"Is he that moody guy who stops by now and then and is gone by breakfast?" said Nick.

Poppy told them they were being mean and stupid. It wasn't her dad's fault that his job took him away a lot and tired him out. She wasn't surprised he got cross with them sometimes because they were very annoying, and always wanting new phones and computer games that cost a lot of money.

"You would say that," said Nick.

"Yes," said Ed. "You're his favourite."

Poppy knew she felt closer to him than they did, but that was partly because of the music. They both loved it. It was her dad who really listened to her piano pieces and understood how hard it was, how disappointing and exhilarating, to learn and play and perform. She often wished he was a cuddlier sort of dad, but then she couldn't imagine Lanky doing a lot of that when he was small. She'd be more of a *Let's-climb-Kilimanjaro-before-lunch* kind of mother.

So Poppy decided her father was doing all right. He wasn't really that much of a grump or a misery guts, not for someone with blanks and question marks and mysteries where his mum and dad should be.

Poppy thought then that time was moving on, and Sorrel the teenage mum who had become her secret grandma was not so young any more. But she had never seen a picture of her, not even a black and white one, or heard anyone say her name out loud.

"Sorrel Golding," she said to herself, in a whisper, in the bath that night. "Don't get too old and die."

Poppy didn't want to lose the grandma she'd never had, not before she understood.

Chapter Two

The summer Poppy would soon be fourteen was different from the start. Her eldest brother, Nick, who had come back from university quite human, rather good-looking and fairly clean, had soon packed and gone away again. Poppy was very proud of him because he'd volunteered to help out in a school that needed rebuilding because it had been destroyed. Another war. There were lots of them and Poppy didn't want to get used to them on screen, grey and smoky and full of rubble and sirens, wrapped bodies and torn faces.

Sorrel Golding was born the year a war ended. World War Two, the big one. Poppy made the connection because it was almost the only fact she knew about her grandma. If Ed and Tim had known, they would have said she was becoming obsessed. Nick wouldn't, because he wasn't mean any more, but he wasn't around to listen to her new obsession. He had his own. He was on the other side of the world, and he didn't phone or email much, but he sent pictures on Facebook, and Ed brought them up on screen so everyone could see. Poppy found it weird because everything and everyone around him was unfamiliar, and even Nick looked altered. Mum said he'd come back changed and Tim said, "Like Clark Kent from the phone box!" but Poppy could see Mum wasn't talking underpants or glasses.

Poppy missed him quite a lot and thought how funny it was the way people changed – a kind of growing on the inside that nobody could track, even the person doing it.

Ed might start changing soon, with luck. He was sixteen and had just finished exams, which had left him in shock and mostly in bed. He rarely emerged, dazed and crumpled, before lunch. Then he needed recovery time online before he could manage a huge bowl of sugary cereal or two. Poppy thought that if she added up the words that stared at her from street signs, buses and shop windows in an average day it would be double the total Ed dredged up for her in a week.

And Tim was on some kind of training camp for people who were mad about sports, especially *high up* or *upside down* sports, the kind that required a safety helmet or a rope, rushing water or sheer drops down into nothing. Poppy had to admit that for someone so exhausting and annoying he was quite brave. Or, as Ed said, barking. And he did yap rather a lot at times, making about as much sense as a terrier.

Poppy didn't mind time on her own, and in any case had plenty of friends, but when Katie and Min both went away on holiday in the same week she remarked to her mum that she might as well be an only child.

"Are you bored, honey?" asked Anna Beth, looking up from her accounts.

"No," said Poppy. "I don't do bored."

Anna Beth smiled.

"No, you don't, do you?" she said. "You're like me that way. Inner resources."

Poppy nearly made some smart remark along the lines of her mother being rather more obviously *in a rush* or *in a muddle*. Still, inner resources sounded cool.

"Can I go and stay with Lanky?" she asked suddenly.

Her mum took off her glasses to think, which could sometimes be ominous. It meant whatever she was thinking about was a big deal.

"That's a surprise," she said.

"We used to visit," Poppy remembered. She'd liked the feel of a donkey's mouth when it snaffled food from her hand.

"Yes," sighed Anna Beth, as if everything had got more complicated and troublesome since. "When you four could be moved around as a set, before you all developed your own different moves in different directions. And before Uncle Derek got ill."

Poppy looked sympathetic even though she didn't remember much about Uncle Derek. Dad had been to the funeral a few months earlier and she knew it had hit him hard.

"Well?" she asked. "Will you ask Lanky? I'll help around the place. She won't have to entertain me." She waited while her mum looked dubious. "Tell her about my inner resources."

Anna Beth smiled. "I'd miss you," she said.

"Call every night."

Poppy hoped her dad wouldn't miss her too much. He wouldn't say, but she wouldn't be able to play the piano for him before she went to bed and the thought of that suddenly made her sad. Still, absence was supposed to make the heart grow fonder.

"Okay," said Mum. "Sure. I'll put it to her."

"Tell her it's a good deal," said Poppy. "And I'll take a home-made cake."

Poppy wondered whether it was the cake that swung it, because her mother came off the phone with a yes which made her feel more excited than she'd expected. She also reached for the cookery book. But it was a complicated recipe and developments went slightly off-target, which brought out what Anna Beth called the *drama queen* in her, the part that pouted, took the whole thing to the bin and had to be stopped from tipping it in. Her mum said Lanky would enjoy it all the more for being a carrot cake without the carrots that were patiently grated and still waiting in the fridge.

"An oddball. Amelanchier Jones will rejoice in a cake like that."

"Has she always been odd?" asked Poppy, realising how good the cake smelt after all and picking a rather delicious fragment from the worktop.

"Eccentric? I think so. Your dad says all the women on his side of the family were unusual." Anna Beth looked for a piece of paper and said they needed a list but Poppy wasn't going to let the subject change, not yet.

"And named after flowers?"

"Yes. A really neat family tradition. I told your dad we must hold on to it."

"So they were unusual but sad?" suggested Poppy, and her mum did her *busy-with-other-things* evasion tactic, mumbling through a packing list. Her only answer, sandwiched between socks and pyjamas, was that she didn't know about that. Poppy wasn't sure she believed her, not entirely, but if she really didn't know about the flower girls, Lanky must. After all, she was one of them.

Poppy knew her dad wasn't sure about the visit because she heard some sort of discussion going on that night which was threatening to become an argument. But her mum must have brought him round as usual and in the morning he said goodbye softly and hugged her as if it really was a big deal, a much bigger one than Poppy understood. It made her tearful after he'd gone.

A few hours or so later Poppy was delivered to the sanctuary with a bulging sports bag, carrying a bunch of flowers from a motorway service station and a few contributions to her bed and board, like digestives and a whole box of teabags.

Lanky was up a tree – "Pollarding!" she cried – in her front garden, and waved a rusty old saw at the sight of them as if it weighed no more than a conductor's baton. She was wearing dungarees and a sun hat, and her face had aged since the last visit a couple of years earlier. She hadn't been a widow then, just a full-time nurse to Derek, but they'd both been cheerful even though they had rather more to complain about than certain brothers Poppy knew.

She seemed pleased to see them and said Poppy's dad (she called him Davy boy) hadn't dropped by for a while. Poppy didn't know he ever did; he'd never said. Anna Beth said he hadn't been working in the area for some time. She was sure he'd visit soon.

"No good expecting a man to pick up a phone," grinned Lanky.

"Why?" asked Poppy, because she really wanted to know, but the two women only shrugged and sighed.

Lanky took Poppy by the shoulders as if to stand her straight and still for inspection. She bit her lip before she smiled.

"Well!" she said, and Poppy waited for a crazy, offbeat comment to follow, but it never did. "Just look at you, Poppy Golding!"

Then, as they dumped everything in Lanky's already overcrowded kitchen, she added that it would be best if Poppy herself never did look. "I'd get shot of any mirrors round the house," she told Anna Beth, "a.s.a.p."

"I know," smiled Anna Beth, who seemed to understand.

Poppy took a moment, but then she smiled awkwardly as she realised what Lanky meant. Not what Ed might mean, which would be an insult to do with ugliness and breaking glass. Lanky meant the opposite. Poppy was pretty; she knew she was and had been used to it ever since old ladies had told her mother so in shops. Could anyone be too good-looking? It was a weird idea. But it struck her that people probably didn't contradict Lanky.

Poppy didn't intend to keep that rule, and she didn't think Lanky would respect her if she did.

Anna Beth had diverted conversation to the flowers in their cellophane and Lanky seized them with a war dance of a whoop. In seconds the flowers became twice as beautiful as her aunt arranged them while she talked. Her mum stayed chatting in the kitchen so long that Poppy wondered whether she'd ever leave. Lanky could see Poppy was itching to go outside and after a while she suggested that she wander out and find a few donkeys.

"Introduce yourself," she said. "Lay down your terms. Firm but fair: tough love." She smiled and Poppy thought her mouth did rather wobbly, donkeyish things. It must be catching. "I'm all talk," added Lanky. "Soft love is what they get. Spoilt rotten, they are."

"They need it, don't they?" said Poppy, rooting out her wellies. "They're ... you know ... damaged, aren't they?"

"Ah," said Lanky. "Yes, they are. Aren't we all?"

But Poppy didn't think she was expected to answer so she disappeared instead.

Like most summer days Poppy could remember, apart from the ones she'd spent in California with her mum's family, it wasn't really hot. Everywhere was moist and green, and in places the ground was sodden, as if it had never really recovered from the winter snow. The pale, streaky sky couldn't make up its mind whether to give the sun a chance, and no part of it could be described as bright, never mind blue. Poppy wasn't really warm enough in her WILD AND FREE T-shirt but she had no intention of shivering like some city airhead who had a thing against wind because it messed her hair. Poppy pinned hers up with grips, in a tumble and spill, mirror-free style, and made her way up to the field, the paddock and the stables.

Poppy remembered her mum calling the sanctuary a mess and her dad asking what she expected of a place coated in dung. She felt unsettled by the thought that he'd been stopping by to see Lanky now and then but never bothered to mention it. Not to her, anyway. But looking around her,

Poppy decided her mother was right. A large skip would certainly come in handy. The corrugated iron didn't help, and the old caravan that Lanky used as an on-site office looked more dilapidated than ever. The place seemed to be full of wheelbarrows tipped up against walls.

As she approached the black wood stables the wind chimes tinkled, reminding her to look over the low wall at the home-made plaques in the donkey cemetery. Poppy didn't remember so many. But of course, she told herself, this place was like a hospice. The last part of the journey. Lanky believed they'd all lived other lives, and would be back, one way or another. She reckoned some of them had been around since Roman times, but Poppy thought that if that was true they'd have had enough long ago and God should say *Enough.*

Reading the names and dates of the departed donkeys, burnt black into sliced wood, Poppy saw how long some of their lives had been (Ziggy, fifty-five), while others had been much too short (Frannie, only nine). She felt Lanky's fondness for them all. Like a doctor in intensive care she lived close to death, and Poppy thought that sometimes, when she wasn't talking, smiling, or laughing wildly, it showed.

Poppy was relieved not to find the name of George among the dead, even though in Lanky's words he'd been well past his sell-by date last time she visited. Poppy was especially fond of the small, spindly-legged roan because he'd been gentler and less frightening than the others when she was tiny. Opening the gate into the paddock, she saw Joss the cat registering her with a brief stare before padding across and lying down in a sunlit patch of dirt. None of the donkeys gathered in the stable area seemed to take much notice of Poppy at first. She didn't want to scare any that might have poor eyesight or hearing, so she called out in the most harmless way possible, introducing herself softly.

One piebald rubbed its backside against the fence. Another walked into a bucket but didn't seem startled. Many of those scattered around stayed still and quiet, intent on being. But the nearest three all stirred at once and moved towards her, heads down to be stroked or rumpled. She used to find that alarming when she felt small enough to fit inside a donkey belly. Now she felt tough enough to cope.

Then she saw George, his colours less than glowing and his progress towards her slow. The others didn't seem too pleased when she transferred her attention, but she liked to think George knew her, even in what must be his donkey dotage. Could it be her smell, or the intonation of her voice? Because she liked to think she looked rather different from the child he'd seen last time.

Poppy counted eleven in the stable area, but saw that in the field that curved up the hill several more were standing, mostly in shady spots, courtesy of trees that edged the boundaries. The big, rusted brown gate was locked but she was sure Lanky expected her to climb it. As she swung herself over, Mo the dog waddled over, her torso rounder and lower to the grass than it used to be, and shook her fluffy head without barking. Officially, she was resident at the vicarage with Lanky's best friends, but she seemed to feel at home among donkeys. Poppy leaned down to muss and chat, but this Mo was a low-volume, more sedate version of the one she remembered and didn't bother to lick her face.

For a moment as she strode up towards them, the donkeys in the field were motionless, like a photograph or an old watercolour in a gallery. Among them was a couple, the jenny small and skewbald and the jack a shade darker and a ruler's length taller. Standing close together like an old married couple in conversation, one leaning in as if to say, *Pardon, love?*, they ignored her so completely that Poppy wondered whether age had dulled their senses, or whether they only had eyes and ears for each other.

Up on the brow of the hill, looking down on her and advancing suddenly, was a jenny even scruffier than she felt herself. But from the eyes it fixed on her she suspected it was not an OAP but a teenager. Its greeting was loud as the average siren. As it brayed it uncovered teeth that were far from pretty, and tangled with green stalks.

"Hullo to you too," she said. "Have you not heard of flossing?"

The jenny didn't look amused.

"What's your name, darlin'?" she asked, careful not to get too close because she knew that donkeys could be nervous of new people or situations.

"Freda," said someone. But although the jaws were grinding as if for conversation, Poppy didn't think it was Freda herself. The voice was deep, even for a difficult donkey.

She didn't see the boy at first. He was in the hut, or rather emerging from it with a bucket. She heard the rustle of loose jeans that straggled over trainers. One bare, bony arm was pulled tense while the other only trailed, but both were long, and more freckled than tanned. His hair was shaved to a soft fuzz that reminded Poppy of a dandelion clock before the wind broke it, but its colour was a faint red blond. In one ear was a pearly drop of a silver stud; around the other swung a hoop with something dangling from it. His nose was turned up, a cartoon kid's nose, but his forehead stretched deep and

28

wide, and his cheekbones were tight because there wasn't much flesh on him. Underneath the egg-like speckling he was pale as the morning, the creamy dawn colour of a sky that hadn't caught on to summer.

Poppy wondered whether he'd looked at her like that, noticing. She blushed at the thought that she'd stared, taking in every long inch of him like a list she had to memorise. But if he'd been scrutinising from the hut, he'd stopped now, and looked away to the donkeys. Freda seemed interested in the contents of the bucket. He patted her muzzle; she seemed used to him, her agitation over.

"What's your name, darlin'?"

The boy didn't quite smile at his joke but Poppy knew he thought he was being funny. Her brothers often wore that look when they were teasing her. It was quite a good impression but he shouldn't have been listening when she didn't know he existed.

"It's rude to eavesdrop," she said quietly, eyes on the donkey.

"I wasn't," he said. "I was just there."

But he didn't explain why. His accent wasn't the same as Lanky's. It took short cuts, knocking off beginnings and ends. Poppy wondered how old he was. Sixteen, like Ed? His jeans hung low like Ed's, as if three other backsides could fit inside them. A small beaded bracelet was tied around his narrow wrist. She thought he must be cold, but she couldn't spot any goose pimples like the ones that were bumping under her own skin.

He moved across to the older donkeys and started to mutter things in their ears. Poppy knew she shouldn't assume he was whispering about her. He'd probably already forgotten she was there and she didn't want to follow him around like a child with a hero.

"You're Poppy," he said. "Like the flower. The one that causes so much trouble."

She'd heard it before, and of course when she was small she hadn't understood. But now she knew what he meant. The drugs trade: big business and endless misery. She'd shouted at Ed the last time he'd made a smart remark because misery wasn't funny. But she couldn't call this boy a stupid, lazy pig. So there was nothing she could say, except *Yes, but poppies are gorgeous too.* She knew enough about boys to realise how vulnerable that would make her.

Poppy said nothing. She just waited, but perhaps the boy wasn't a big talker. Except, of course, to donkeys, and that seemed to be a private conversation.

"Who are you?" she asked in the end, feeling a little jealous because the donkeys showed so much more interest in this boy than in her. For the first time she realised that he must be kind because they trusted him.

"I help out," he said.

"I can see that," said Poppy. "They like you."

"Impeccable taste, donkeys," he said, hurrying the adjective. "Seen what they eat?"

She smiled. She couldn't remember whether she was wearing mascara. And there was nowhere to check the wildness of her hair, but she found herself fingering it like a comb.

"You didn't think I'd know that kind of word," he said. "You look fine, by the way. Not impeccable, but fine."

30

Poppy didn't want him to think she cared either way.

"Auntie Lanky didn't say you worked here," she said, looking away to the hills where the sun was battling through.

"Just a volunteer really," he said. "Sort of. Got addicted."

"Oh," she said weakly.

"To the mud and smell."

"Ah," she said, wishing she could edit out these non-words that were all she could find. "I'd better go."

The boy took no notice. He was ruffling the donkey pair just where they liked it, around their ears. Poppy headed back towards the house, a little sudden warmth stroking the back of her neck. She heard herself all the way, wellies rubbery, ground squelchy. Ed had told her she didn't walk like a girl and she'd said models on catwalks couldn't walk at all; they looked like they hadn't been screwed together properly and limbs might drop off. Her friend Min had a pair of four-inch heels she couldn't stand in, never mind walk. Poppy was pretty certain this boy wouldn't have watched her now even if she'd been in a red mini dress and thigh-high boots.

"I'm Kane," she heard behind her.

There must be all sorts of smart remarks, thought Poppy, *that I could throw casually over my shoulder.* Naughty boys and canes. But smart remarks weren't really her style. She'd rather talk straight, like Lanky.

"Oh," she said.

When she looked around at the gate she couldn't see him. Wondering whether he was watching her from the hut, she walked on. Her face felt rosy now. It must be the wind.

She walked quickly past the stables, mumbling affectionately to the donkeys that were too slow to butt her this time. Then she almost ran to the house. Taking her boots off at the back door, she found her mum hugging Auntie Lanky goodbye.

"Kinda cute," said Anna Beth, in what Poppy called her *best U.S. teen.*

Poppy gave her a hard look that judged her tone, her accent and her words as well as the spying. Then she reflected that without her glasses all her mother would have seen as far away as the top of the field was a stringy blob. So she was fishing. Poppy decided to pretend she hadn't heard.

"He's all right, young Kane," said Lanky. "In fact he's actually very able."

The two women laughed as if they'd been drinking wine instead of a whole pot of tea.

"Biblical references will be lost on my daughter, I'm afraid," said Anna Beth.

"What?" asked Poppy, feeling shut out and young. Her mum said there were two brothers called Cain and Abel and one killed the other.

"Cain was the murderer," said Lanky. "But this Kane is spelled differently, and wasn't such a good citizen in the past." From the laughter Poppy could tell this was another story she didn't know. "But he's rehabilitating well."

"Poppy's not much of a film buff either," said Anna Beth, and told her *Citizen Kane* was a famous, classic movie from way before her time. "But don't ask me for a plot summary, because I haven't seen it for thirty years and I can barely remember what happened yesterday."

"Yesterday," said Poppy, "you said the same thing."

Anna Beth looked at Lanky, who smiled and said it must be nice to be young. Poppy gave her mother a look that wondered whether she was going now.

"I'm off, honey," said Anna Beth. "Be good."

Poppy's raised eyebrows meant *Mum do you have to?* Anna Beth apologised as she kissed her cheek. She hung on tightly as if she might not see Poppy for another six months instead of three days and Poppy remembered how tearful she'd been when they'd waved Nick off at the airport.

She stood with Lanky and they watched Anna Beth reverse out of the ridged, muddy track that ended in the house. She narrowly missed the tree that supported a washing line where sheets dragged out towards the stream.

Lanky yelled at the back of the car so loudly that Poppy flinched. "Remind Davy I'm still here, will you?" Then she put an arm around Poppy's shoulder. "I'm glad you're here, Poppy. I really am."

Her aunt looked from the old bike leaning in the hallway to the swollen black bin liners gathered in the dining room ready for Oxfam. She ran her fingers back through the short, mannish hair at her temples, which was dark grey and woolly, with variegated white veining through. Her cheeks were a rather sore shade of red, and her eyebrows were growing a bit too close. But she looked like someone who mattered. An inventor or an artist, or an archbishop on a day off.

"But you're much too beautiful for your own good, you know," she added, as she put her hands on her narrow hips. "If you were my daughter, I'd keep you locked up. Now, where did I put the secateurs?"

Poppy shrugged and smiled.

"Don't mind me," said Lanky. "I get nuttier. Good carrot cake, by the way. Now that you're here we'll have flowers round the house again. Move on. Funeral over. Buds and shoots, you know? It was clever of you to guess."

"I like flowers," said Poppy.

"Of course you do," said Lanky, with an *ah!* that suggested she'd found what she was looking for. "It's in the blood. Like the beauty. Exactly like her."

"Like who?" she asked. Everyone always said Poppy looked more like her dad than her mother.

"Oh, ignore me, Poppy. I chunter on. I'm not used to censoring myself for other people. Derek gave me free rein, bless him." She looked at Poppy.

"That's love, isn't it," asked Poppy, "accepting people the way they are?"

"Oh, it may be, Poppy. But it's ourselves we want accepted, isn't it, and other people we want to change?"

"But who am I like?" Poppy persisted, reluctant to let Lanky off with diversionary tactics.

"Maybe more like me than you'd choose, with a bit between your teeth, not letting go!"

She followed her aunt out into the garden where roses climbed a wall, their petals scattered on the dark earth beneath like confetti at a wedding. The smell was amazing. Lanky clipped and passed them back to her one by one, until she was holding five of them, stripped of thorns and beaded with night rain.

"These will jazz up those conservative ones you brought," Lanky said, "and get them dancing!"

"Mmm," said Poppy. "Roses are great dancers, aren't they?"

"Great singers! Great artists! Such performers!" cried her aunt, taking a deep breath as she straightened herself up.

Back indoors, she invited Poppy to slip the roses into the vase and shake things up. Poppy hesitated.

"There's no big secret to arranging flowers," she told her. "Hang the theory. WILD AND FREE, that's all, like your T-shirt. Ears and eyes and heart on full. You'll feel it."

So Poppy had a go while Lanky bustled about. Then she turned back to her aunt with a smile because she knew. She'd done it. Lanky laughed and told her she was a natural.

"Is Kane a natural?" Poppy asked, watching Lanky search for something as if only turning the kitchen upside down would help.

"Ah," she said, "Kane's a conundrum. Not so easy to read and that's the way he wants it. No one gets too close without a mane and hooves. You mustn't let yourself be fascinated, Poppy, not by him."

Poppy didn't like that. It was teacherly and mother-like and not what she expected from Lanky. Poppy sat down at the table with one hand under her chin. With the other she flicked a cake crumb around. The drawers shut with a shove and Lanky sat down opposite. She gave Poppy a searching look.

"Bossy old bat," she said. "Sorry."

"That's okay," said Poppy, who thought she had been getting better at forgiving people. "Don't do it again!" she risked with a smile.

"I wouldn't want anything to spoil our few days," said Lanky. "And I'd rather talk about you than Kane Bradley or even roses. I want to get to know you, Poppy. It's late in the day but important. Will you let me?"

Poppy could have used the *why?* word, but she worked out her own answer. Lanky had no children, her husband was dead and her sister was a question mark.

"So how shall we start? I don't like chat show interviews. Silly, skimmy froth. But then again you won't want a grilling. You'll just have to tell me what you want to tell, and reveal the rest like a character in a book – in action."

Poppy must have looked unsure but Lanky patted her hand and told her not to panic.

"Action! Plenty of that round here."

Lanky had a list of possibilities and Poppy considered them. Muck-raking could wait. Shopping sounded urban and jam-making a bit too hot and sticky.

"I'd like to get to know the donkeys," she said. She listed those she remembered, starting with George.

"Ah, George! I swear he's older than I am! When we were girls we used to stop and stroke him, long before this place existed. It was cruel to keep him on his own like that, the way Mac Trandle did, but I don't think people were so aware then how sensitive donkeys are and how lonely and depressed they can get. There might never have been a sanctuary at all if it hadn't been for George."

Poppy wanted to learn all their names and stories. Having ridden one that was almost white when she was small, she remembered the fear, the smell and the sway, the bump and wobble, the excitement and pride. But the OAPs didn't look as if they'd be inclined to budge an inch for any rider and Freda would probably rather wrap Poppy's hair around her teeth and pull her along by it.

"I don't hold with riding as a rule," Lanky told her. "It's the last thing most of them want. But they're all different ..."

"I don't have to ride," Poppy put in quickly. "I'm not a child ..."

It trailed away lamely. Spot the giveaway! Who protested like that except children? Poppy was used to Nick and Tim grinning together whenever she reminded them of her age as if she was a five-year-old telling the world she'd be six in three months and twelve days.

"Oh goodness, I can see that! Although why everyone's in such a fired-up hurry to leave childhood behind's a mystery to me! As if the teenage years were anything but a trial and a severing ..."

Poppy began to ask what that was all about, but Lanky was ready now, keys and phone collected, boots located. As they walked across she mentioned that Kane would have clocked off.

"One day he'll have the manners to say goodbye."

"You're not big on manners," Poppy pointed out, and Lanky laughed aloud and said she was guilty as charged.

They passed the donkey graveyard and through the gate to the paddock and stables.

Lanky introduced each donkey as they all milled around, and told her how each one liked to be stroked, patted or tickled. Misty, who only turned her head, had been lame, infested with worms and suffering from rain scald when she arrived. Stardust was petrified of trailers because she'd been dragged around so much, first on photo shoots for promotional work and then from one market to another in search of the highest possible bid. Pinball Wizard had been skin and bones when Lanky bought him, his feet sawn short with a hacksaw. Poppy couldn't believe the horror stories but she had the feeling Lanky didn't think much of people. Joely's undershot jaw would cause problems with eating later on in life and Jerry, who had been in such good condition that he'd been intended for meat, was now the noisiest donkey in the sanctuary. As he proved in a conversation in which Lanky upped her own volume but couldn't compete.

She opened the gate into the field, calling softly to a very small jenny that poked her head from out from the lean-to as if suspicious of the sunshine breaking through. A couple of rabbits darted through the bushes into the copse on one side of the field, distracting Poppy with the whiteness of their tails and their speed and bounce. The sanctuary was a slow place, thick with age, caution and fear. It wasn't magic Lanky worked. Healing took time.

"Midge had enough rides to last a lifetime," she told Poppy. "Beach donkey. Bored out of her brains, back and forth, year after year, long after she was ready for a rest. And in between seasons, left to rot. Found her chained up, knee deep in her own mess, old stagnant water in a bucket and grass worn to mud."

"That's so evil!" cried Poppy. "Poor Midge!"

But which one was she?

"She hides," said Lanky. "All this space and she doesn't go far."

There wasn't much space to the side of the hut but as they crossed towards it, Poppy noticed a mottled, ragged

38

shape filling it. The head was tucked in blindly when it could have reached over the hedge.

"Here we come, Midge," called Lanky, gently. "Only old Lanky and a friend."

She slowed down and kept making chirruping sounds all the way, edging closer. Poppy noticed one crusted eye, and another sore not quite healed. She kept behind her aunt, only afraid that her unfamiliar breathing and stranger's scent would make the donkey panic.

"There," said Lanky, arm around Midge, who nuzzled in. "One old girl to another." She patted the patchy coat and stroked the mane. "She won't be with us long," she told Poppy, "but I want her to venture out, feel the breeze, trust the sunshine, you know? If we ever get any."

"Wilder and freer?" suggested Poppy.

"Exactly."

The way Lanky said the word made it sound warm and breathy, like *I love you*. Midge was stirring herself like a cat in front of the fire but still asleep. She adjusted her feet without actually moving, just repositioning. Her hooves could do with some kind of polish. They looked as if they'd been eaten away from the inside, like the donkey herself.

"We'll try," said Lanky. "I've tried every day for a week."

She made sure she was close enough for Midge to feel the warmth of her breath as she backed away, calling softly, hoping Midge would follow. But she didn't move. No easing or edging. Just all four feet firmly in place on the worn grass between the shed and the hedge. Midge was staying where she was, in her corner.

"I want to tempt her out without the bridle and reins," Lanky explained. "She's had enough of them. I've tried food of all kinds but she isn't bothered. Something of an eating disorder, our Midge. An anorexic donkey."

Not far away, but in a different mood altogether, the old couple were still together. Mary and Ben.

"Ben's OCD," said Lanky. "Counts on routine, a bit like a husband. And he's not as dozy as he looks. He has bursts of energy in between dreams, don't you, Benjamin?"

He was one of the pair and knew his name when he heard it, stirring into an alertness that was almost frisky. Mary raised her head.

"That's Mary," said Lanky. "Late-life love."

"Really?" asked Poppy. "They really are a couple?"

"Well, they seem more affectionate than most old marrieds," said her aunt. "Bit past any hanky panky, though."

Poppy thought of a joke but she didn't ask the question: *Don't you encourage hanky panky, Lanky?* Poppy knew what hanky panky meant. It sounded more fun than snogging or any of those words for sex.

Ben and Mary might be a bit old for that but most people would say Sorrel Golding had been too young to have a baby with no husband around.

"Dad thinks I'm too young to have a boyfriend," she told Lanky, as they left the lovers alone.

"I should think so!" snorted Lanky. "He's hit the nail on the proverbial head and I hope he hammers it hard!"

"I'm nearly fourteen!" protested Poppy.

"Innocence and experience," said Lanky. She greeted Mo with rough affection as the dog slotted herself between the two of them, three scampering steps to each of Lanky's paces. "Songs of. William Blake. Good title for a poetry collection, except that with experience most people stop singing. Sing while you can, Poppy. Once you've stopped you'll miss the music."

Poppy frowned.

"Can you explain?" she asked.

"I never explain!" cried Lanky. "Work it out!"

Poppy wondered whether things with Lanky were likely to go smoothly. Personally she felt a few corners rubbing and poking out already.

But it was a good afternoon. Later, before supper, they walked in the woods. On the way, down the lane, Poppy spotted a kestrel above a wheat-stacked field. She watched it, hanging fire without a shadow, and time seemed new. In the woods themselves they saw a single, high-speed hare with an athlete's stride, one muntjac and a stream of deer led by a stag. They followed the brook and listened to the water mounting pebbles and tumbling through the weir. Poppy decided the country had lots of inner resources and they were all free.

She was so exhausted when she went to bed that night that she thought she'd do an Ed and sleep till afternoon. But the bed felt high and narrow and dated back way before Ikea, its firmness supported by some kind of metal, and the sheet tucked in around a peachy blanket that felt thin as well as tickly.

As it was, she woke again before midnight and stared at the darkness, inside and out. The house had its creaks and the bed made most of them as she prized herself out of it. But the world it belonged in was as quiet as Lanky had warned her it would be, and when she crossed carefully to the window she was shocked by the thickness of it. No street lights, no station platforms running along behind lit-up shops, no cars shining a path in the distance, winding down through black to brightness. Just emptiness with stars scattered across it like daisies in a field.

Where are you, moon? she asked, head between the curtains. They were old and faded, the buttery yellow of the cotton blotted pale as cream in places. Who had slept in this room before her? Who had eased down under the blanket like a page of A4 into a see-through wallet?

"You look exactly like her."

Not like Mum at all. She looked like Sorrel Golding. That was what Lanky had meant! And Sorrel had loved flowers too. Poppy felt cold beside the window and made her way back to bed, managing to stub her toe on what she thought was the metal leg of the frame. Gasping bravely so as not to wake the neighbourhood with a scream, she realised something was poking out under the bed. She knelt down and felt underneath, her fingers catching some fluff that gathered floatily like cyclamen in winter.

It was a picnic basket. Her fingers recognised the rough weave before her eyes adjusted. Poppy pulled it out and lifted the lid to a papery smell, a feathery kind of mustiness. Among the loose pages, some of them folded, was a book, a soft one, like a wallpaper catalogue, almost too big to fit in the basket. She pulled it out and realised it was a photo album, from the days when people had the patience to stick on corners and tuck the pictures in.

Poppy reached back to the wall and found the switch on the lamp stand. She pushed it in and sat on the bed with the album on her lap as close as possible to the light. Her dressing gown was on the end of the bed so she put it over her shoulders in the hope that she'd stop shivering.

A baby boy, looking grumpy, and then a girl, in a flower-head kind of hat frilled like petals. Two children in play clothes, the girl a nurse with a red cross on her bib. The girl with a doll hanging from one hand as if its china arm would snap off.

When were these taken? After the war? A mother with lipstick and a best dress that showed her figure. A looker, film star-ish, with hair that might have been shaped by what her mother called a jello mould.

And the girl again, no longer busy and unaware of the camera, too old now to be caught while she was just being. She was posing this time, staring the camera out, not quite smiling but amused, maybe by herself. Tall and thin like Poppy, hair long and thick like hers, some of it dragged across her face by a sudden wind. Not a woman yet, but beginning to become one. No make-up, but lovely. She wore high-waisted trousers and a tucked-in blouse, and she was standing up to her ankles in bluebells. Even in black and white there was something hazy about them, melting into a gauze.

"Sorrel Golding," Poppy whispered. "Is it you?"

And if it was, then the grumpy baby boy was poor Joe who hadn't lived to see Lanky born. And the little girl holding her hand in the next picture over the page was Amelanchier herself, looking up with a smile that meant this pretty big sister in a party dress with a bow at the waist and a ribbon in her hair was, in that moment anyway, the love of her life.

Poppy knew she wasn't meant to be looking even before she heard the step on the landing. Her aunt had seen the light under the door. She shoved the basket back under the bed with a scrape that might have been heard in Wales, shrugged off her dressing gown and slid into bed.

"You all right, Poppy?" came the voice.

Poppy switched off the lamp. She edged deeper down under the blanket and pushed its hem away from her chin so it wouldn't tickle.

"Fine!" she called thinly.

"Night night," said Lanky, and Poppy heard her bedroom door creak shut.

"Night!" she called, feeling sneaky and excited at the same time, and closed her eyes.

Chapter Three

Poppy heard the rain next morning before she saw it. Waking to its fingernail prick on the glass, she remembered where she was and asked herself why everything in this other world sounded so different, even rain. It looked different too, misting the hills and sapping the colours. The sky itself was a feeble yellowing grey, like old skin. But there was a lushness, a softness in the air when she opened the window. She felt as if a moment's sun would be enough to transform everything as dramatically as the winter snow.

Kane. She'd dreamed him, donkeys ringing around him, joining like a furry ribbon. Better not mention that to Lanky.

A song swelled from the shower. The singer must have been waiting to hear her stir so as not to wake her. *All the lonely people ... Where do they all come from? All the lonely people ... Where do they all belong?* But Amelanchier Jones didn't sound mournful. With a voice that was big and bluesy, she was more of a diva than a widow in a church choir.

At breakfast, looking out on rain still beading the window, Lanky said she could have showered outside and scared away the crows. Poppy sipped the dark, strong coffee and smiled at the thought of her auntie in the rain without her clothes.

"I was never remotely beautiful. Once I told my mother it wasn't fair to give a girl a flower name and expect her to live up to it." Lanky laughed out loud. "I told her she should have called me Cuckoo Spit or Knotweed!"

Her shake-shoulder laugh was the catching sort and Poppy nearly blew coffee bubbles through her nostrils. Lanky wiped the corner of an eye with a thick middle finger.

"Poppy suits you," she said. "I bet you like red."

Poppy told her she did, and described a dress her dad had bought for her birthday when she begged. A dress that was too good to wear, and yet she'd packed it with tissue paper and hung it up in Lanky's wardrobe as soon as she'd arrived.

Lanky was spreading honey into butter on toast. It reminded Poppy of the bricklayer who had built the extension wall at home. She might have been slapping cement.

"That beauty I mentioned," she told Poppy. "Don't let it be a curse."

Poppy was about to bite her own toast but she waited, slice in the air, eyes fixed. Maybe she could will the explanation out.

"It always has been, for the flower girls," continued Lanky, but she sounded reluctant. "The ones who had it. It's not exactly an accident but it's not exactly a gift either. Not that I'm speaking personally of course. But you can trust me on this one. It's hard to outshine it, you see, inside out. People get dazzled. You can't escape your own reflection."

I know who you mean, thought Poppy. *You're talking about Sorrel. Tell me. Tell me everything.*

Lanky's mobile phone bleeped a text. Her shoulders sank. Then she stiffened them and replied, muttering

46

impatiently about the slowness and mistakes which she blamed on technology.

Ed would ask *What technology?* He'd call it a brick.

"We'll have to let some workmen in at the school, I'm afraid."

"Oh. I thought ..."

Poppy knew her great uncle Derek had been caretaker until he became too ill. Apparently Lanky was a kind of a sub when the new one wasn't around. Dad had pointed out the school once, driving past on a visit, because he'd been there too. But she had a feeling about the generation above him on the family tree ...

"You went there when you were little, didn't you, Lanky?"

"Oh yes, long ago. Worlds ago, Poppy, believe me."

Sorrel went too, before her. So Poppy decided she didn't mind seeing the school at all, even though she'd been counting on seeing Kane.

As she put on her trainers she looked out of the window towards the field and hut, but trees and bushes joined with the hedge and fence to make spying impossible.

"No Kane today," said Lanky.

"Oh," said Poppy, and hearing herself, thought how much one non-word could betray. If she'd realised she would have practised a more casual delivery.

"His little sister isn't well and he has to look after her because his mother can't take time off work."

"Oh," Poppy managed, a little more neutral this time, even though she was thinking that Kane must be a nice big brother, and hoping that he wasn't sprawled in front of the telly or computer, ignoring the sister or snapping at her. She pictured him reading her a story instead and realised both scenes were equally easy to imagine.

But she only had two more days. Suppose the sister wasn't better tomorrow?

Wildwood School. Poppy thought it was a great name. GIRLS and BOYS were still carved above the two doors where they used to line up and enter separately, and although there were modern extensions, Lanky said the Victorian part looked almost the same on the outside as it had done when it took all the children in the village, all the way through. But Poppy had worked out that because of the seven years between them, by the time Lanky was top of the juniors, Sorrel was an unmarried mum. And when Sorrel was one of the big girls in the playground, Lanky was too young for school.

Of course the playground had more colour now, with plastic play equipment of all kinds, and a garden with a sandpit and a growing arch of willow for the infants to run through. Surprise sun brightened everything; the dampness shone and shadows stretched in a crazy array of shapes. There was a Wendy house that even Queen Victoria's children would have died for. Poppy didn't suppose playtime was as much fun in Lanky's days, but her aunt wasn't so sure.

"We never got tired of skipping. Different rhymes and different rules. You'd think these long legs would get tangled, but I was the champion. Unbeatable."

Lanky was unlocking now. There was a code and an alarm. As they went inside Poppy thought how strange schools felt without children. There were no hot body smells, no faint whiffs of crisps from lunchboxes or cheesy feet. It was quiet, too, with no electric murmurs from computers or whiteboards or photocopiers to throb softly through the papery air. No chain of footsteps trailing down from the hall. It felt like an office, but all the doors were shut, no fingers were tapping or clicking, and even the radiators had nothing to say.

"Not very wild today," said Lanky.

Poppy remembered the photograph of the two sisters. They didn't look wild at all. Good girls, more light than darkness. Sun without shadows, and golden summers.

The camera couldn't lie. She'd heard that somewhere, but she knew it wasn't true. There was a special, posed picture at home that proved it – of her, sitting leaning against Ed. He was doing the cheeky, gap-toothed grin he always turned on when he was about nine, when in fact he'd just thrown a massive wobbly. He'd been furious about having his hair brushed and wearing a particular jumper instead of a football top. It didn't show. Under the surface was a heaving swell of anger at having his photo taken, and he stomped off straight after the button had been pressed and threw his jumper on the floor. But only the surface showed. There were no traces.

Were there lies in the photos of Sorrel Golding under the metal bed? But even if there were, it seemed to Poppy that silence was the biggest lie of all.

"Can I explore?" she asked Lanky, who was jangling keys and trying to find the one to the secretary's office. The phone rang and they heard it go onto answer machine. A van turned into the car park, spreading Radio One out of the open window. For a building that was closed it was getting rather busy.

Poppy wandered off down the corridor, past the untidy bookcases and the laminated reminders of how to behave. Past the empty display boards with corrugated edging flapping away from staples, probably tugged by grubby fingers filing by. Up some steps she strode, three at a time, feeling oddly adventurous and slightly illicit. A spider plant from high above children's reach sprouted and trailed to a brittle crisp at the end of its tentacles. A shedding aspidistra gasped for water, the earth around it shrinking away like a sooty sandcastle ready to tip out. Poppy turned another corner into the cloakroom, which was littered with small, left-behind shoes, not all of them pairs, and P.E. bags that wouldn't smell too good by the end of the summer. But Poppy wasn't really interested in the children who'd be back in September. She was thinking about pupils who left a very long time ago. So she was heading for the original centre, the 1868 beginning around which the extensions had been added.

It was the dining room now and a residue of onions and gravy lingered behind. It was as if it had accumulated over decades, disinfectant-proof, and soaked through the stone. The chairs were wipe-over plastic these days, but the walls, with their high, stained glass windows, were of Victorian brick, over-painted again and again, chinks covered over, cracks filled in. There was a shield and a motto in the coloured glass, but Poppy's Latin consisted of Status Quo and that was only because her dad once did an embarrassing dance at a wedding to a song called *Rocking All Over The World* and her brothers had never let him forget it.

At one end of the dining hall was a board listing those who'd won scholarships, whatever that meant. She checked the dates. No Amelanchier. But her big sister was there. The last name on the list, painted in perfect lettering. Sorrel Golding, 1956. She'd been a clever girl, a star pupil.

But something had gone wrong. Beautiful, unusual and clever hadn't been enough to stop her being sad.

The sun burst so strong and warm through the stained glass that colours gathered shining on the floor. Poppy stepped into them and let the rainbow fragments decorate her hands. She tried to imagine what the room would have looked like without the electric lights and the plastic. She pictured wooden desks in rows, a blackboard squeaky with chalk, a stove with a guard around it, and a cane at the ready. A schoolmistress in black, with spectacles on the end of her nose, looking severe the way her own class teacher hadn't really managed to do on Victorian Day when they'd all dressed up and pretended, but giggled a lot more than Victorian children ever dared.

Tamarisk Freer. She heard the words as if someone was calling a register in her head. Where had they come from? For a moment Poppy thought it was the workmen's radio. But she realised how silent the room had become, as if the door with its alarm and the secretary's office with its ringing phone were miles away. Or years.

"Tamarisk Freer!"

It was sharp this time, imperious, a reproach. Poppy turned all around as if she'd heard footsteps in the dark. Nothing. Then the sound of something hard rapping a wooden surface.

Boots creaked in the doorway. The girl who wore them was long and thin, but her feet weighed down in the hobnailed soles that had brought mud with them, mud she was studying fearfully. As she looked at the floor, her hair fell from a loosening ribbon meant to keep it from her forehead. Her pinafore was white but she wiped a smear of dirt that refused to be shifted. Poppy pictured her walking through woods and a wet branch leaving its mark.

Not for one moment did Poppy think she was in costume. But the stirring she felt was not alarm.

The girl was Poppy's age, and Poppy's height. She looked cold, in spite of the shawl over her shoulders, but her cheeks reddened as she bobbed and held out her hands. The swish and the thwack came instantly, and unsteadied her a little, like wind around branches. Her head hung, eyes on her boots. Then, four strokes later, she moved slowly to her place in a row, on a bench facing a tilted wooden surface, a slate lying bare in front of her.

Poppy felt her own breath rise and shorten as if it might stop. The girl was the centre of a scene like an illustration in a book. But the scene was torn at the edges, as if the page had been ripped away from the binding and was floating in water. Around it, bright, tough and shiny, lay 2009, the present surrounding the past as if it was a stray fragment left behind. And in spite of the tightness, Poppy felt no fear. It was as if she'd accepted an invitation, arrived, and now simply observed.

The girl set her mouth in a line she held firm. Tears pricked her eyes with brightness.

Not my fault, you witch.

She didn't hear the words, but she tracked them to the forehead where the fair hair fell astray, the forehead looking up now towards the front of the class. She saw no teacher, no fellow scholars, no one else. Just Tamarisk Freer, thinking thoughts that only she could read.

Cows to milk and all of them prettier than you, with sweeter breath.

Tamarisk stood in a hurry, smoothing her pinafore and trying to restrain the hair that spilt in front of her eyes.

"Empress of India, Miss Teale."

Approved, the girl was allowed to sit.

See, she didn't think I'd know. She doesn't like it when I get the answers right. She looks like she's swallowed something nasty. I wonder what she'd say if I told her the old Queen had no business ruling India, and that my papa says the Empire will soon be nothing but a shameful memory of arrogance and tyranny.

Poppy stared. Tamarisk was looking at her. Her mouth was closed in a small smile of satisfaction that a correct answer had spared her further reprimands, but her eyes, which were blue, and framed by thick sand-blonde lashes, were fixed on Poppy as she sat down again and laid her hands on her lap.

Time women got the vote. I wrote to Mrs Pankhurst, to thank her for her courage and determination. My mother's a Suffragette too, a fast woman. My papa says the village can't keep up with her.

It might almost have been a film, the kind she enjoyed most. Poppy liked history, especially when women grabbed lead roles for themselves instead of clapping the men from

53

the audience, or pampering them backstage. Now she knew that a hundred years ago, more or less, a flower girl called Tamarisk Freer had walked to this school every day, and blossomed gloriously, only to be punished with the rod. Poppy did the maths. This was her great, great grandmother. And what she felt was a wild kind of readiness.

The quietness was brittle now. As Tamarisk gripped the pencil, it dragged across the slate in a muted screech that seemed to break from inside her and multiply, as if she was the first violin in the orchestra and the rest were echoing in unison, following her lead. A chorus of strokes on slates gathered into a surging forte of scraping sound, like a storm advancing, drawing closer, about to break. And from the invisible chests of the scholars around Tamarisk breathed a linen thickness, not quite soft, of secret sighs. Poppy felt as if she was eavesdropping on their longing, their swelling to burst free from the letters they could only copy and the words they could only repeat.

Tamarisk moved her arm. On the slate she had written a message, in a loose and not very even loopy hand. It was a message to which her eyes directed Poppy with wide and bright intent.

I languish in captivity.

Please, I beg you, set me free.

Slowly, with a discreetly placed sleeve, Tamarisk rubbed the words away. As she did so there was a creak and a snap.

For a moment Poppy thought the rod had swung down hard on flesh. But the dining room door opened and there was Lanky, filling the space almost to the top of it. The air warmed, the faintness around Tamarisk filled out in bold and the scene at the core of everything was torn away like a

blotted page to be attempted again. And all that was left was
a flurry of wind from nowhere that seemed to breathe a word.
Sorrel.

"There you are!" said Lanky. "I've been hunting for you
everywhere."

She looked questioningly at Poppy, who wondered
whether something showed, and if so, what it looked like.
Her aunt narrowed her eyes in a way that was a joke rather
than an accusation.

"What have you found, Poppy? What have you been up
to?"

"Nothing," protested Poppy, realising she sounded
defensive, like Tim when he'd kicked a ball that had just
flattened a sunflower. "I've just been imagining."

"You've been looking at the photograph over the old
fireplace," guessed Lanky, as if she'd just remembered it. She
strode down to the far end of the room where it hung, black
and white but a little brown, and muzzy as a sleepy child.
"I've often wondered whether one of those girls in pinafores
is my grandmother, Tamarisk Freer. What do you think?"

Poppy followed, steadying herself, breathing as deeply
as she could. Together they studied the picture with its three
rows of children, none of them smiling. Poppy wondered
whether instead of inviting them all to say "Sausages!" the
man behind the camera on a tripod with a black hood had
instructed them to chorus an elongated, nasal "Dooooom".
The schoolmistress looked as sour as month-old milk. Miss
Teale. It had to be. Her face was wide and flat, as if a cartoon
frying pan had struck it. Poppy imagined Tamarisk wielding
one in her dreams.

There she was, in the back row, taller than any other girl, fair and willowy, pale and beautiful in spite of the emptiness of the expression she'd pulled across like curtains. Tamarisk. No mistaking her, even though she looked older now.

"Look at the attitude on this one," said Lanky, pointing to her. "A teenager before teenagers existed!"

Poppy nodded vigorously, not sure she could speak. Her aunt shrugged and muttered that if it was Tamarisk, the date would make her fourteen.

"We'll never know, I dare say."

"It's her," said Poppy. "I'm sure it is."

She wished she could make the girl in the photo smile. She realised she felt muzzy herself, the way she did after a long sleep. That was the explanation, had to be. Of course.

"What happened to her?" she asked.

"I wish I knew," Lanky told her, turning away so that Poppy had to follow, and leading her back to the door. "She died when I was tiny. All she meant to me was the picture my sister kept by her bed." Her face tightened out of the smile. "Time to go."

As the hall door closed behind them, Poppy felt as if she was leaving the cinema with the credits rolling. Fantasy over. All the way back along the corridor she watched her aunt's shoulders, the swing of the long arms and the slight flap behind of the spotty sunhat that didn't belong with the jeans and working boots.

Sorrel. Like a chorus it was back – the final word, and with it the trapped breath. Again and again Poppy asked the question silently, in different tones. And then she forced it out like a blurted protest, a challenge or demand. Without the

56

please. No pause between sentences. Petulant, complaining. All wrong.

"Tell me about Sorrel before I go. I need to know."

Lanky stopped. Poppy half-expected her to swing round and stare, but she didn't. She stood still and straight, pausing just for a brief moment before the next stride. When she took it, it was longer than ever. The answer was flung back on the move, hard and fast, like one of those serves in tennis that no one can return.

"You don't. You need to hang on to your ignorance. Believe me. And if you can't, I'll take you home, right now, because I can't help you, not with that. All right?"

The question was almost aggressive, almost a threat from an *EastEnders* heavy. It meant, *Shut it!* It meant *Enough.* Poppy felt her mouth lose shape and hang, an angry sob starting to form behind it, just as trapped as her breath had been.

"What's the matter with you?" she yelled in her head. She drilled it into Lanky's back.

Lanky turned this time, as if she felt the words strike. She blew out and her hands went to her narrow hips, where they rested a moment, as if she needed to hold herself firm and still. She looked back at Poppy with something like a squint, evasive, unable to hold the gaze.

"I'm sorry, Poppy. It's that tough love thing. Non-negotiable, I'm afraid." She tried an unconvincing smile. "I didn't mean to bite."

Poppy looked away at the display boards. They were careless and scrappy. Depressing. They were bare of everything but leftover staples, some of them angled like spiders' legs and some trapping specks of coloured paper behind them. It felt as if they were all that was left of a picture she'd painted in her head, colourful and interesting, until Amelanchier Jones tore it down.

Poppy had hoped Anna Beth might be right about growing up, and finding it easier to forgive things – the stupid, thoughtless things her brothers said or did. But at that moment she couldn't imagine herself forgiving Lanky for ripping that portrait away. She wasn't the person she'd pretended to be, and all that rough-edged honesty that people had to take or leave because directness was right and true was just a sham. What was more dishonest than pretending to be open and wacky and different and then slamming down the rod like Miss Teale?

I hate you. Poppy's brothers had teased her with it, when she was little, and made out it was her catchphrase, always exaggerating the tears in it when they made fun with their impressions. And Poppy thought it now, for a step or two down the corridor, her own strides shortening as Lanky's lengthened, so that she fell further and further behind.

At the next fire door Lanky waited, holding it open for her. Poppy kept her eyes lowered as she walked through. She wasn't going to smile just to make her aunt feel better. Like a toe stubbed on a sharp corner of furniture, the hurt still throbbed.

She had to wait while Lanky answered the phone again for a brief conversation with a man who'd come to replace a door. Wandering off in the other direction towards the Nursery, she passed a display case with a handwritten, folded over sign inside it, naming the local historical society. Around it were photographs, a very black coal bucket, a hoop and a doll, an embroidered Christening gown and a few coins with Queen Victoria's head on them. There was even a cane of the kind that Miss Teale must have used, lying harmless, with no traces of flesh or blood. But what interested Poppy most were the books, large and dark and leathery as old bibles, with pages brown as tea. LOG BOOK, they said, and somebody had stuck paper labels on them with dates. 1877. 1895. The most recent she could see was 1911. Poppy felt certain Tamarisk Freer must be in one of them. Maybe her daughters were there too. Maybe Sorrel Golding was mentioned somewhere, and if not behind that glass, where?

"I fell asleep," she told herself, out loud.

It sounded more convincing than the alternative, "*I saw a ghost.*" She hadn't slept well in Lanky's metal bed. She'd probably seen that photograph on the far wall straight away, without registering it, and it had nestled deep down in her imagination. Her head had been full of the past and the sun had warmed her into a dream, a daydream, a let's pretend game of the kind she loved not so long ago when she operated on her dolls, lined teddies up for assembly and encountered aliens in the garden.

What would Katie and Min say if she texted? *Just met my great, great grandmother in a haunted school.* What would Kane think?

Lanky was back, her cheekbones less pronounced now that chatting had loosened her, the smile bright until it wasn't returned. Poppy didn't care any more. She wasn't the one who had thrown the friendship away.

"Where are the other school log books?"

Poppy knew her tone was still stroppy, a little resentment hanging on. Lanky shut some doors and told her she didn't know, but they might be in the Head's office. Then she unlocked it, clattered huffily with grunts and sighs, and emerged again. In her hands were three heavy volumes, their binding hanging loose. They smelt musty. Poppy wondered whether some sort of permission should be applied for, but didn't ask.

"These do as a start?" she asked, handing them over.

Poppy nodded but didn't thank her. They climbed into the car.

"I know I upset you, Poppy," she said, sitting back when she'd been just about to start the ignition. "I'm ashamed of myself, snapping and snarling and throwing a moody on you. Bereavement's no excuse and I'd be cowardly if I hid behind it."

Poppy felt the forgiveness roll her over like a wave. That was what she expected. No adult high ground, no resting on the right not to explain or the claim that she was too young to understand. Just *fair cop, banged to rights*. The Lanky she'd trusted.

"Look," continued her aunt, pulling off her sunhat and grimacing in the driver's mirror at hair that was flattened and hadn't yet sprung back. "No, not at that unsightly spectacle! Look, Poppy, it's all a bit of an open wound. The past, I mean. A family tragedy, you might say. Our roots go deep round here, but they're tangled and not so pretty, and they're destructive too, the way roots can be."

"You mean they pull houses down."

Lanky nodded and started up the engine. Poppy realised that was it. End of subject. The only explanation she was going to get. But there had to be more. As Lanky looked to the left to turn out of the school drive, Poppy saw a brightness in her eyes that was fierce but sad. Her aunt looked the other way and kept her eyes, wet or dry, on the road. Poppy touched her arm. Her turn to feel sorry now.

"I know she's your grandma," Lanky murmured, as if she was talking to the steering wheel. "Was. Is. Could have been. You never met her and that's a loss ..."

"But you lost your sister."

"I did. I have. And I loved her with a passion, you see. She was my favourite person in the whole world and she broke my heart."

"I'm sorry."

"I'm not as tough as I look. But don't tell." Lanky exhaled. "Maybe if it was over, I could draw a line. THE END. But it's all unfinished, ends untied, mystery unsolved. Past seeps into present. And contaminates." She pulled her mouth down, donkeyish again. "Don't let it infect you too, sweetpea. Leave it alone, eh?"

"I'll try."

It wasn't much of an answer but Lanky let it go. Poppy reckoned she'd decided to respect her for avoiding promises she might break.

The mobile on the dashboard bleeped. Lanky reprimanded herself for failing to turn it off and asked Poppy to take a look.

"*Back now,*" she read. "*R U on way? Midge in funny mood.*"

"Kane," said Lanky, and Poppy clicked down.

It was. He was back. She felt a surge of something warm and bird-like inside. It was like the feeling she'd had when she'd played her favourite Grade Four piece, the Chopin prelude, the best she'd ever played it, and her teacher had smiled and told her it was gorgeous. Only that time the bird had lifted off and this time it felt trapped and a bit dazed. *Get a grip,* Lanky would say. And really, she'd have to agree.

But Poppy wondered guiltily what kind of funny mood Midge was in. Maybe she'd seen a ghost too: The Ghost of Donkeys Past. Everything felt rather silly and unstable, inside and out, and she was in danger of giggling inappropriately or opening her mouth on nonsense. But Lanky was taking it seriously. She looked anxious and told Poppy to text back that Kane should call the vet if he was in any doubt.

The reply suggested *Shrink more use?*

Lanky tutted.

"Mental health," she said. "Still a joke. Poor old Midge."

Lanky might be nuts, thought Poppy, but she didn't talk about meeting ghosts. It was nothing. It was a screenplay. When her dad defended her to her mum after she'd been extreme, he said she was creative and sensitive and that was why she played piano the way she did.

The way Lanky was rattling along the lanes, they'd soon be back, and Poppy would see Kane again. Not that he'd be fluttering too.

Chapter Four

Poppy saw the buggy first. There were mud marks where the feet banged, fragments of crisps wedged into cracks and one hair bobble lying grubbily at the back of the seat. A small child with a padded bottom tilted up like a duck about to dive was examining wildlife around her flowery boots.

Registering the sound of the engine, she scrutinised them with eyes narrowed against the sun and shouted, "Lanky!"

She was pointing at the driver. The child shouted again, stumbling over to Kane, who was carrying chaff. He put it down and ran to take her hand, pulling her aside to allow plenty of room for the car.

"Not sure what Health and Safety would make of this, Kane," remarked Lanky as she stepped out. She smiled at the girl and told her, "I'm Mrs Jones. You must be Lol. Pleased to meet you."

Lol's stare was a little suspicious. She was freckled like her brother, but pinker – apart from her mouth, which was red as watermelon and just as moist.

"Lanky," she said, firmly.

"So it seems," said Lanky, with a narrow-eyed glance at Kane, who pointed the finger of blame at Poppy. "I can't have Lol near the donkeys with an infection of any kind. And

I can't have your mother suing me if she eats something she shouldn't, either."

"She's fine now," said Kane. "She did eat something she shouldn't, but that was yesterday, and at least we didn't have to go to A and E this time. But I haven't let her near the donkeys." He paused. "And my mum's not the suing kind."

"Glad to hear it," said Lanky, and Poppy could tell she was anxious to see Midge. She told them to stay there. Then her pace almost sped to a jog as she headed up to the field.

Kane lifted his sister into the buggy and strapped her in, ignoring her barrel-chested attempts to burst free. These efforts were accompanied by a grunt, which seemed to gather in a nose that was much too small to contain it. Her face reddened with straining, even after he managed the final click – which didn't stop her kicking.

"All right?" he asked Poppy.

"Mmm," she said, even though it was more of a greeting than a question. She wondered what he'd say to a full and truthful reply.

"See why I'm good with donkeys," he said. "I practise with Lol."

She was still kicking, but stopped to stare up at Poppy.

"Laurel?" Poppy guessed. "Or Lauren?"

"Just Lol. Like on texts. I didn't know what it meant for ages."

"Lots of love," she said, and hoped she wasn't blushing even though her mouth curled up towards her dimples in sudden embarrassment.

64

"Yeah. My mother's what you'd call an individual. A loved-up individual. She got married again just before Christmas." He offered her some gum which she took with thanks that were almost swallowed. "Are your parents still together?"

"Mmm," she said again, feeling lucky in spite of that family tragedy Lanky had mentioned. Whatever the past concealed or revealed, for the moment her present felt full of summer light and colour, and a kind of excitement that couldn't really be dangerous.

"You get used to things in the end," said Kane.

"I got used to my grandma being a question mark," she told him suddenly, "but now I'm determined to find out why."

He smiled. She thought he might be laughing at her. Did she sound very young?

"Is it a quest?" he asked.

"Quests don't have to be mythical," she said, pleased with the word, "or involve dragons. Any more than poppies have to destroy lives. It's people who do that. So yes, it is. A quest."

He smiled again.

"Do you make a lot of speeches?"

"You asked."

"It was good," he said. "I'll help if you want."

Of course she wanted, even if he didn't really take her seriously. But she couldn't be sure how he'd react to anything, least of all ghosts. After all, he couldn't be so different from Ed, and Ed would throw his head forward and

65

squish his nose and mouth together as if he couldn't believe his eyes and ears. As if she was a joke, a very bad one.

"Thanks," she murmured.

If Kane had a strategy for the quest he didn't have time to outline it, because Lanky was shouting. Poppy ran ahead while Kane revved up the buggy into careering mode, which wasn't very successful given the wheel tracks and bumps. Poppy couldn't be sure whether the shout was anxious or excited, for help or an audience. As they hurried up to the field, she heard braying that was screechy with stress.

The hooves pounded like a show jumping soundtrack, but frantic and directionless. Lol screamed. Midge wasn't behind the shed. Uncaged and wild, she was twisting as if she might catch her own tail and tear it off. But the energy that spun and wired her was spent in seconds. It ebbed away like a retreating tide, leaving her still and weak, staring emptily, saliva bubbling at her open mouth.

"All right, girl," muttered Kane, leaving the handles of the buggy to Poppy and opening the gate very gradually. "All right now, Midge. Soft and slow." He drew closer. She backed away. He reached. She stepped back again, her snort high-pitched, but stopped. "Soft and slow. Very soft and slow."

Kane laid a hand on Midge's back and left it there until her head stopped turning and her eyes dulled their glare. Poppy felt a rush of relief and tenderness.

With her eyes on Midge, and on Kane alongside her, reassuring still, she saw Lanky only in the corner of the frame, but knew at once. No stride. No colour under her eyes. She was hurt.

Lanky hobbled towards Midge, her tongue clicking the soothing sounds Poppy had heard the day before. Poppy stared at the leg she was dragging in a limp and hoped Lol couldn't see the blood dark through her jeans. Kane edged back, unlatched the gate and stepped back on the other side of it, the side that separated safety from danger in a way Poppy hadn't imagined it might. She knew her eyes must have been wide with alarm as they connected with his.

Kane fumbled for his mobile and took a few steps back to use it. Still Lanky was calmly stroking Midge, murmuring, head to head, trying for eye to eye. Poppy turned Lol away from the blood and towards her big brother, who waved once or twice during the call. Then he came to take the buggy, while Poppy closed the gate behind them.

"Vet's coming," he said. "Ambulance too. Poppy will go to the hospital with you. I'll stay here. Don't argue, all right?"

"All right," agreed Lanky, her voice someone else's.

"Does it hurt?" asked Poppy, feeling stupid as soon as she'd asked.

"Fuss about nothing," snorted Lanky, and tried to grin. "This lad's getting too big for his boots. Soon be bossier than I am."

"Do you want to sit down?" he asked, and she stopped and jerked down onto grass, leg straightening with difficulty. She lifted it underneath as if it was wooden and separate from her.

"Poor old Midge," she breathed. "I should have seen it coming."

"What happened?" asked Poppy. In the silence that followed she realised she was still asking why.

"Fetch her some water," Kane told her quietly.

She hurried off to the house, kicked off her boots and tried to calm her brain into recognition of everything. Water. A mug. She lifted her eyebrows at her stupidity as she searched for one without a chip or stain, grabbed the nearest and let the tap run cool.

Poppy saw the phone there on the worktop and called her father, left a message and stumbled back into her boots. In her head she heard the account she'd given on the voicemail and the reaction Lanky would supply if she heard it herself. *Donkeys never bite. Practically never. No such thing as a rogue donkey. Just rogue people.* What had happened to Midge to make her stop cowering and attack? It was horrible. A horrible day, one act of aggression after another. First Miss Teale, then Lanky and now Midge, and she hadn't imagined any of it, because none of it seemed possible. Boundaries hadn't just shifted; they'd upped and redrawn themselves without consulting anyone.

What would she do without Kane? Cry, of course. Cry continually. Out-baby Lol, who seemed to embrace everything in her wide-mouthed gaze. Ask to go home. Wish she'd never come. Drama queen.

But it wasn't a holiday any more. She'd be needed, really needed. She and Kane. And he was going to help her too, with Tamarisk and the other flower girls. Poppy hoped they could help Midge too, because she had a feeling Midge would cry if she could.

Lanky, of course, chose not to. The power of her resistance held her gripped as she lay on the grass, her breathing shallow. Kane was talking, focusing her on other things. Lol distracted her too, pointing and naming, not always clearly. Poppy wanted to join in, but a ghost story might not be good for her great aunt's health, and nothing outside her unfamiliar new world of donkeys and Victorian schools seemed to matter now.

When the ambulance arrived she went with Lanky, who seemed to know the brother of the driver and apologised for being feeble and not making her own way to hospital. As they turned out towards the road Poppy looked out at Kane, afraid to smile inappropriately but careful not to look too anxious or lost. He lifted Lol's hand to wave, and she waved back. His wink was a warm surprise that took its time to melt through her face while she looked away.

The bite was not as deep, and the stitches not as many, as Poppy had feared. Infection was a risk and Lanky was told that whatever her feelings about medication she must cooperate religiously. The doctors and nurses were shocked that a donkey had bitten her.

"It's the first case I've ever seen," they all said, one after another.

"You won't let the vet put Midge down, will you?" Poppy asked her.

Lanky managed a snort. "What do you think?!"

"Because it's not really her fault if she's disturbed, is it?"

"Certainly not," agreed Lanky.

"Will you text him and say so?"

Lanky said it wasn't necessary but in the end she gave Poppy her mobile with the vet's number on it, and permission to ban the death penalty.

After all the waiting around and stupid celebrity magazines, Poppy was glad to step outside and enjoy the sunshine. Avoiding the smokers, and trying not to engage with the awful hopelessness in some of the faces, she sent the vet's message and wished she'd given Kane her own mobile number. Imagining his voice, and the account she'd give him, she checked down Lanky's contact list with her thumb. Kane wasn't there. Disappointed, Poppy took out her own phone and called her father.

"So you're all right?" he checked at the end of her news bulletin.

"Yeah, I'm fine. Can I stay longer, Dad, because Lanky's going to need me more than ever now?"

He supposed so but he'd talk to her tomorrow.

"Dad, you know Tamarisk Freer?"

The pause was so long and full that she might as well have asked whether he knew that her mother had another husband and family in the States.

"My great grandmother. I never knew her. Why?"

"Was she always unhappy?"

"She must have been, to leave her husband. Women didn't do that then."

At last! Information! And not just a date or a photo but a big episode, the kind a village would talk about for months, years. Poor Tamarisk.

"Did he beat her or something?"

"How old do you think I am? We're talking a hundred years ago! Poppy, this isn't really the time. And don't ask Lanky, not when she's poorly. All right?"

"Mmmm," she said. She could tell he wasn't satisfied with that.

"I'll come and see her in a day or two. Give her my love."

"Is she buried round here?"

"What! Leave the past alone, Poppy. You've got enough on your hands in the present."

It was true, but Poppy felt more excited than daunted. She could stay longer, she could find records and graves, ask and research. She had log books to examine, next time she had a fortnight to spare. And she had a promise of help from an able assistant. He'd been so cool in a crisis. And he'd winked at her.

That was how a short stay turned into a summer. And how floodgates of a sort opened wider than she might have dreamed. In a way, of course, Midge did the opening, bursting out of her hiding place like an armed, revengeful prisoner when Lanky had been trying to coax her out into freedom. As the vet said, a case of biting the leg that fed her.

Dan the vet was young and scruffy, in a smooth expensive way. His long, rather glossy hair had to be tucked behind his ears at regular intervals, in a way that troubled Poppy because of where his hands might have been. Lanky, who was supposed to be resting her leg, invited him round the day after the incident to discuss options – as long as he

71

understood that donkey death was not one of them. Kane had dismissed him as *upper class* before he arrived, and he did sound like an American attempting the accent as if English people all had a double-barrelled name and socialised with Prince Charles.

Dan had an idea about Midge. Lanky had often used acupuncture and homeopathy, but never tried Bach flower remedies, which certainly seemed to Poppy the most romantic option. Lanky nodded excitedly.

The sun was verging on hot, so they sat outside at the picnic table Great Uncle Derek had made. Poppy tried to ignore the bird droppings streaking it, and buried the nearest one under her mug. It turned into a meeting with the arrival of a large, overdressed man in a corduroy jacket and shiny pointed shoes, referred to by Lanky, as he shifted his weight from the four-by-four, as "the money man". As he raised a hand in greeting and lumbered towards the garden, a loud "Haloooo!" came floating like the call of an exotic bird soaring over his head. It came from the path behind, where a petite woman was chasing him in heels.

Poppy remembered Natalie but she'd forgotten her clothes. In a tight summer vest and short denim skirt she leaned in to kiss the money man on both cheeks before speeding past him to embrace a folding Lanky on tiptoe.

The largest part of Natalie was her wild, shaggy perm, which would have hidden her gold hoop earrings completely if they hadn't been the size of coasters. Her skirt exposed veined bare legs, one of which was ringed in an ankle bracelet that tinkled. But as Lanky introduced her, Poppy saw that in fact, in spite of the eyeliner and blusher, and the 'age 13' label that might well be tucked under the waistband of her skirt, she was Lanky's age. They'd been friends for ever.

Poppy made a pot of tea and brought it out on a tray with what was left of the carrotless cake. Natalie, who looked as if she never ate anything containing more than eleven calories, ate a large slice in seconds and licked around her lipsticked mouth with noisy relish.

"Dreamy, Poppy," she said. "You can come and stay with me any time."

The money man was called Geoffrey, but he was on a diet. He watched everyone else eating. They talked business and accounts for a few minutes and Poppy could see Kane was bored. But she could also see, from the way he licked his finger and used it to pick up crumbs, that he liked her cake. Lanky was making notes on the back of an envelope, which she called the minutes of the meeting.

1. Lank to behave (if poss)

2. K paid extra hours

3. Nat domestics

4. Geoff fork out for therapy for M

5. Dan investigate options

6. P stay on (and make more cake)

As Poppy read them, Lanky grinned.

"Richard Branson learned all he knows from me."

Dan said he had to go but would check on Midge on his way out. Kane got up and Poppy decided to follow.

"Don't go in that field, you two!" called Lanky. "I know it was a one-off – of course it was – but even so ..."

Dan assured her they'd watch from the other side of the gate. He led the other donkeys out towards the neighbours' field, which was on short-term loan, but wasn't so large or so green and seemed to be overrun with spurge. One by one, Dan delivered them through the gate for Kane and Poppy to escort them in. Only Freda seemed disinclined to budge and Poppy remembered the idea that donkeys were stubborn. But Freda didn't seem to know; a carrot was all it took.

"Freda, you're so easy!" said Kane. "A stereotype!"

All the while Midge remained hidden, and although Dan kept an eye on her he didn't go near.

Finally, when the others were settled, he went to find her, back in her corner behind the hut. She was wedged into the smallest possible angle, so that Dan couldn't get all the way round her and gave up trying. Midge was very quiet, like a storm that had exhausted itself. Poppy watched and listened from the other side of the gate. She couldn't quite hear what Dan was saying but Kane whispered that he was probably telling her *behaviour of that sort jolly well wasn't on and she'd better pull her socks up. Old girl.*

Then Kane swung his long legs over and walked steadily over to the hut. Midge didn't seem to notice and Dan didn't bother to send him away. Poppy felt trapped. If she did the same Dan would send her back like a child, and if she stayed where she was Kane might think she was behaving like one.

"You were here, weren't you," she heard Dan ask, "when the old girl lost it?"

For a moment Poppy thought Dan was talking about Lanky and wondering how he knew about her tantrum in the school corridor. Then she realised he meant Midge, and was talking to Kane. But Kane wasn't answering. While Dan moved slowly away from Midge, he was shuffling, eyes on the hills.

"You were with Midge just before she threw her wobbly?" persisted Dan, moving towards the gate.

"Sorry? Are these specialist medical terms?" asked Kane, in the end, without looking up.

Dan scrutinised him. Kane was still avoiding eye contact. Suddenly Poppy understood. She felt indignation swell hot inside her somewhere. Kane didn't look hot. He had stiffened from the mouth down, his shoulders, his arms ... He was icy.

"I meant ..." began Dan.

"You know I was here."

Poppy heard the tightening in Kane's voice. It must have been contagious because she felt it through her own silence.

"I'm not suggesting you were to blame in any way. I just ..."

"You just thought that since I'm some kind of community payback thug I probably poked her in the eye with a stick."

Kane looked up at last, but she couldn't be sure whether the colour in his face and the nip and tuck of his mouth were defiant or hurt. She didn't know him well enough. She didn't really know him at all.

"I wasn't suggesting anything, mate." Dan tried to sound casual, like a big brother rather than a teacher. "I was just looking for clues, that's all."

"I can't help you," said Kane. He looked sideways at Poppy. "What is this, Cluedo?"

She supposed a joke meant he was loosening.

"Just so you know, Kane," said Dan, who seemed instantly more comfortable, "Mrs Jones never said anything about any kind of community payback. She told me you were a young friend helping out."

"Oh."

"You accused me of making assumptions ..."

"You did," Poppy pointed out. But rather than appreciating her support, Kane gave her a look that told her he'd handle this, thank you. He looked back to Dan and shrugged.

"I made assumptions too," he admitted.

"Yes."

Dan stretched out a hand, probably not that clean but no dirtier than Kane's. Kane looked embarrassed, but shook it.

"Quits, then," added Dan.

As the vet drove away Poppy called him a snob. Kane stared after him a while and she thought something was still festering.

"*Just so you know,*" he said, in a scorchingly accurate impression that upped the aristocratic content of Dan's long slow vowels. He paused while she giggled. "I'm not community payback. I haven't buried my overalls under the hay and I'm not tagged. All right?"

"You said it," she said, defensive. "I didn't."

"It's a long story."

"Most people's are."

He seemed to be considering that.

"Natalie's might be epic. Or a one-liner. But I do know she's the vicar's wife. Believe it or not."

Poppy's forehead creased. She told him she did know that! She'd known Natalie (slightly) since she was tiny.

"Clues, sleuth! Quest?" he continued. "Churches have records, right? And graveyards." He shook his head as if he despaired. "You need to watch more repeats on daytime TV."

"Will you tell me the long story before I go home?" asked Poppy.

"Shouldn't think so," he said.

But he didn't sound annoyed, or even certain.

"I'll speak to Natalie," Poppy told him, and there she was, on cue, rising from the picnic table, pulling down the skirt that had ridden up as she sat, and waving at them.

"Poppy!" she called. "Come and help me get some shopping in."

Kane lifted his eyebrows as if he'd planned the whole thing and expected her to be impressed. She smiled at him. He was difficult to read, but she decided she liked trusting him.

"Kane will still be here when you get back!" cried Natalie. "Plenty of muck to keep him busy."

Poppy didn't quite blush, but she did wish adults didn't have to behave that way. She mooched off to join her with a quiet "Bye!" thrown behind.

Natalie was shorter than Poppy even though her hair extended her height by at least ten percent. She elbowed one arm, inviting Poppy to slip hers through. They walked away together, but Poppy didn't find it easy to keep in step. She wondered if the size of Natalie's heels accounted for the hip swerves.

"Poor Lanky! It's a good thing you're here to keep her spirits up. She loves those donkeys to bits, you know, and the more broken they are the more she wants to mend them. So she's taking it hard."

Poppy realised she must be.

"Were you really at school together?"

"Oh yes! We were the chatterboxes. Some things never change, eh?" Natalie looked pleased with herself, as if she had just told a rude joke and couldn't help finding it funny.

"Are we going back to the vicarage to get your car?" asked Poppy.

Natalie said that was the plan and hoped a young thing like Poppy could manage a few hundred yards.

"No problem," said Poppy, briskly. "Can we go through the graveyard?"

Chapter Five

The church was small and low, like a cabin, and seemed so much a part of its surroundings that Poppy wondered whether it had sunk stony old roots deep into the earth. Grass sprang up spiky, reaching towards the windows. Natalie said it was not as old as Nature pretended – a mere thousand years – but it needed work and a lot of money if the bell tower was to be saved. Only big enough to house a single bell, this looked to Poppy like a jigsaw piece that didn't quite fit. Natalie blamed wind, sun, rain and birds, but mainly time.

"Fund-raising is in what you might call full swing," she told Poppy. "We'll get you running a cake stall if you don't look out!"

Poppy made the right noises, but although she hoped the church had a future she couldn't help being more interested in the past.

"Natalie," she began, and hoped she wasn't interrupting the details of the action plan, "can I have a look around? I mean, do we have to get the shopping straight away? Have you got things you need to do?"

Natalie smiled and searched in a patchwork shoulder bag. Its mirrors caught the sun as the tassels swung. She produced a bunch of keys and separated a large brown one that looked as if it could open the door to a dungeon.

"I know!" laughed Natalie. "If a key could talk I reckon this one could hold an audience. It's stiff, and you have to pull the old door towards you as you turn. Just lock up again when you've finished. I'll knock off a few emails and be back in half an hour." She handed the key to Poppy. "Is that long enough?"

Poppy thanked her, but as Natalie wound a path through to the vicarage hidden behind trees and bushes, she turned away from the small low door and walked back towards the graveyard.

In summer brightness it was anything but creepy. With so much plant life it was more like a garden with stone features, a kind of crazy paving with carvings and mounds. A willow trailed shade. The border along one side was thick with heleniums, rudbeckias and black-eyed Susans, bold and brazen, gold and red. A theatre of fire, thought Poppy, and wondered whether repeating the phrase out loud would make her crazy. As peaceful as tissue paper flames in a school play, they were backlit not by wiring but by sun. And pastel-pale hollyhocks edged the walls and paths, reaching up past her waist like a crowd at a wedding dressed for the photos. There was a scattering of vases bright with roses, freesias and chrysanthemums, all of them fresh, as if whoever had arranged them there came every day to keep remembering. Poppy didn't suppose Kane could name the flowers, but perhaps his dad had taught him other things.

It was the flower names on the gravestones that mattered more. Poppy could have asked Natalie where they were, her ancestors, the ones she needed to fill in on the tree and in her imagination. But it felt important to find them herself.

Some were hard to read, obscured by erosion or lichen. Some were sadder than anything should be: a baby who lived from 1811 to 1811, and three brothers who died under twenty-one in the Great War, their graves empty because their bodies had been left behind in Flanders. Unlike the donkeys, these people were commemorated at somebody's expense. At the head of one flat marble slab she noticed an angel, almost Tim's size. It was dulled and drizzled by birds and rain, but its erect, symmetrical wings had survived intact. Black and masculine, this was a powerful angel for an important man. Poppy moved closer and read his name in sharply angled Times Roman letters.

ROBERT HENRY MADISON, she read. 1881 – 1933. Gentleman and philanthropist.

There was no word of any wife or children, and although there was more than enough space below for a lengthy poem, or a Latin epigram, the rest was bare apart from a few scroll-type decorations in the corners.

I forgive him now.

The words were like breeze. Poppy could not locate them in the weeds or brambles, stinging nettles or hedge. She looked to the angel, but he was as stern as ever, his mouth set hard. This voice was young, almost familiar. It sounded the way she heard herself on recordings, rather breathy and uneven, less assured than she sounded in life.

A girl put her arm around the angel's wing, and patted his rigid curls. A different girl this time, a girl on cue and no surprise. She was developing like a negative in a photo booth, her dress darkening, the tips of her shoes fuzzy, her fair, loosely plaited hair not outlined but haloed vaguely as if against blinding sun.

Poppy could have squeezed her own flesh very hard or slapped her warm cheeks. She didn't bother. She knew she couldn't will or reason it away.

He was my father and I hated him. One day in the school holidays when he was at the office my mother told us to pack the things that mattered and we left. We thought we were going to the seaside, but we did not return until he died.

The accent changed from phrase to phrase, strong then light, rising and ebbing away. Poppy understood. The mother she meant was Tamarisk. Tamarisk Freer had married Robert Madison, left him and taken their children to France. But which of them was this, and where was she going? Shapeless in a kind of tunic dress and sensible shoes, the girl was walking now. Her long arms swung like Lanky's when she strode, leading Poppy past the graves. She stopped at a small stone, grey and simple, with no marble and no angel. Someone had left flowers in a bulb-shaped vase.

TAMARISK MADISON, it said. 1890 – 1955. Brave and beautiful mother of Hebe, Camellia and Celandine, John and Arthur.

The girl knelt down on her skirt, and leaned towards the gladioli. They were riotous, but she was pale: a watercolour wash of an image, a different medium. She reached out a finger, but not to touch the flowers. Hebe was pointing to her name.

I loved her. She was magnifique. She gave us music – Beethoven and Bach and Schumann and Chopin, stormy and creamy. Just tears of the sun, she'd say. Music and flowers, always flowers, as we opened the door.

The voice of Hebe Madison. She was Poppy's great grandmother, the link to the world she knew, the intersection.

But why had she hated her father? What could she not forgive? And where was Hebe buried, if not here?

One moment Hebe knelt at her mother's grave. The next she had gone, thinning like smoke from a fire that had died to ash. Poppy looked around, as if like a butterfly this girl had flown away to land again, and she only had to find her. But Hebe had left. The sounds of cars, bikes and pedestrians surged around the churchyard as if power that had been cut was now restored. The last raindrops fell from the branches above Tamarisk's grave as a breeze flapped the notices in the porch.

When would this stop? Poppy had a feeling it was a beginning. She knew she should be afraid, but what she felt was curiosity, and it drove her the way she liked to be driven.

The church key still hung from her hand. She felt it suddenly, indenting her skin. She hurried to the door and remembered what Natalie had said, pulling it as she turned. With a clunk and a creak it scraped open and she was inside, where it was cool and the stone was not soaked by sun, or misshaped by lichen, but curved by hands and dipped by feet. The pews were dark and low, carved with busy, writhing crests and scenes. The windows were small and plain, with no text, drama or rainbow spills. But Tamarisk would have approved of the flowers. They were everywhere, threading their scent through the time-dust and emptiness, welcoming her, celebrating the now.

Had all the flower girls worshipped here, married here, christened their babies, been carried in coffins along the narrow aisle? Everyone but Sorrel. And what had happened to her baby, Poppy's dad? Was this where David had been given his name, and *one baptism for the forgiveness of sins?*

Poppy felt the closeness of the past like a flood of winter air inside her.

The organ that struck up the Wedding March was faint at first, like a lost dream elusive by daylight. And this time she drifted into it so passively that it might have been another episode, airing on schedule. Through the door, which Poppy had left open to the sun, stepped a bride on the arm of her mother. They had the same smile, and each wore a single lily, the bride's pinned to her cream dress, the mother's to her dark red suit. As they moved through the church, Poppy glimpsed the spaces where the crowd should be. The shifting, soft-edged scene flowed like water on wood, slow and spreading towards her. But highlighted at its centre were empty places.

Was it wartime? At first Poppy saw no men, no khaki shoulders, and no hair that wasn't long, piled or hidden under a best hat. Then the slight figure at the front turned with a smile that opened wide, a boy's smile, shy but overwhelmed. In a suit that dropped loose around his body, he waited for his bride, who wore no veil to hide the difference between them.

Poppy heard the vows in snatches, the way she heard the Radio 3 announcers on a motorway. Hebe Madison vowed to love, honour and cherish Paul Golding, and he vowed to love, honour and cherish her, as long as they both should live.

And as the two of them left the church she heard Hebe's voice through the Handel, still laced with Paris, but stronger now, a woman's voice. Poppy felt as if she'd been waiting for it, arrived and put a coin in a slot and there it was, on demand. Because she was controlling it, wasn't she, still directing?

He was an evacuee who joined the choir, only fourteen when he arrived from London, and I was twenty-seven already. He was just a boy to me, but three years later, when we met again at a concert, I fell in love. Then the war began and Paul declared himself. A conchie. Between us, we received a lot of letters, my mother, my lover and I, the vicar too. We could have torn them up for confetti and left the words lying like blossom. Coward. Immorality. Shame. Oh, and Punishment. And Hell.

The music surged. Hebe's head turned, surrounded by sun in the doorway, and she smiled as she stepped outside on Paul's arm. Sudden silence cut – frayed – through the church. Poppy felt alone, and cold.

Then into the porch stepped Natalie, hair first, letting the light through her curls and waving.

"Ready, Poppy?"

Poppy couldn't find her voice, not immediately. She made her way up the aisle like the wartime bride and through the heavy door into brightness. She found herself looking down as if she might find paper fragments scattered and waiting on the grass, among the daisies outside the porch. Words of outrage and hate.

Poppy knew she couldn't make this up because she didn't know; she couldn't have begun ...

"Interesting?" asked Natalie.

Poppy said it was. "Is Hebe Golding buried here?"

Natalie didn't seem surprised. "No. I believe she was cremated. Her ashes were scattered in her garden, on the flower beds. Nothing to see, I'm afraid."

"Except the flowers?"

Natalie smiled.

"I can understand you wanting to know, Poppy. I'd be the same. But Lanky is my dearest friend and she's had to hold together all these years. I'm not sure that she's ready to have the past dug up like a body for an autopsy. Do you see?"

Without waiting for an answer, Natalie took the keys and locked up. She dropped them in her bag and gave Poppy a look that made her feel analysed, evaluated. She was trying to get her colour back, her flesh and blood and certainty, and she needed time.

She felt no sense of danger, but she recognised a kind of dread, because she didn't know where this was leading. Whether she could stop it by giving up on the truth, or whether something had started that she could not abandon and there was no longer a choice.

"Live your own life, Poppy. A church is more than graves and records. The sun is shining. And you're a flower girl!"

The light and the colours were strong. Poppy's eyes burned. She thought Natalie must have noticed because she put an arm round her shoulder.

"Believe me," she said, "that's a great thing to be!"

Poppy believed her. She slipped into Natalie's small red car and reran it all in her mind: the rich father, the musical mother, the boy husband who wouldn't fight. She was almost startled when Natalie put on a rock compilation CD and sang along badly, but with plenty of movement at the wheel.

They did the shopping, crossing off Lanky's list, stopping first at an organic farm where they stocked up with large root veg with the earth still clinging on. Then they moved on to a small supermarket. Natalie seemed to know most of the people serving and buying, and introduced Poppy to some of them. Poppy thought it was a bit like trying to shop with Madonna, except that people stopped her for health updates on other villagers rather than photos or autographs.

Then a grey-haired man waved, hurried over, looked intently at Poppy and introduced himself as a retired teacher who had taught her father geography. He wanted to know how David was.

"He's fine," she said, and felt suddenly sad, because she wished her father would let her know him well enough to answer.

As they returned to the sanctuary with the windows wide open, Poppy decided to take a chance. Natalie had turned up the volume. Her hands beat a rhythm on the steering wheel and her head kept the same time, side to side, up and down.

"What's a conchie?" Poppy asked suddenly. "You can tell me, because I know that bit already."

Natalie told her to turn off the music.

"A conscientious objector," she said, "refused to join the armed forces on moral or religious grounds. Conviction. Many of them were Quakers. They had to contribute in other ways, but first they had to prove their case."

"What do you mean?" asked Poppy. "How? Did they go to court? Were they on trial?"

"In a way. It wasn't easy to opt out. People spoke up for them, as character witnesses. They faced a lot of hostility because people thought they were cowards, or taking some kind of moral high ground." She smiled at Poppy. "I don't know how you found out, but maybe you can be proud of your great grandfather. It took a different kind of courage and he was very young."

"I am proud," said Poppy, and asked who'd spoken up for him.

"There's someone who might be able to tell you more about that," Natalie added as she parked. "Leave it with me."

"Thanks," said Poppy, looking out for Kane. There was no sign of him up on the field as they unloaded. She was afraid that they had been too long, and he'd gone.

"Hullo," said a voice behind them. Kane reached to help her with the bags. "All right?"

"That's hard to answer," she told him.

"Say hmmm," he advised. "That gives nothing away."

She smiled, shy again.

"Can you two manage?" asked Natalie. "Tell Lanky I'll call in again this evening."

They both said *yes* at once.

Kane had been about to leave, but stayed long enough for Poppy to show him what she knew, sketched on a piece of printer paper. She was too rushed to make it artistic, but the family tree was looking a bit less spindly. At the kitchen table surrounded by shopping, she talked him through and then recapped.

"Poor Tamarisk Freer married Robert Madison."

"Who was filthy rich but evil," he butted in.

She hoped he was taking it seriously. "So she ran away to France with the children and didn't come back until he'd died."

"What happened to Camellia and Celandine? And the two boys?"

Poppy said she didn't know yet.

"But Hebe married an evacuee-turned-pacifist, how many years younger than her?"

"Thirteen," she said.

"People shouldn't have numbers by their names."

"Of course not!" said Poppy, but that seemed like a big subject and she wanted to stay focused. "I hope they were happy."

"Don't count on it," said Kane.

Poppy wanted to argue, but if they were, their happiness didn't last forever. Their daughter Sorrel saw to that, even though Poppy was sure she didn't mean to. Kane looked away to take a text. She knew he assumed Natalie had told her all of this and she didn't correct his mistake. He seemed impressed. But part of her wanted to tell him the untellable.

Then Lanky, who was online in her office, called for Kane. He saluted for Poppy's amusement and took the stairs two at a time. By the time Poppy had unpacked, he was hurrying down again and leaving with a casual "See ya!" from the doorway.

"Poppy!" called Lanky, louder than she needed to be. "Come and tell me what you've been up to!"

"Coming!" she called back. She remembered Kane's advice. *Hmmm* might come in useful.

It was a while before Poppy had the opportunity to make a start on the three log books from Wildwood School, beginning with the earliest, 1900 – 01. She remembered that Queen Victoria died that year and found a reference to mourning, and celebration of the new king. The writing was so slanted and loopy it was very hard to read, but she could make out the words 'National Anthem'. She imagined all the pupils standing straight in the school yard with the flag flying, and Tamarisk taller than the rest around her. Tamarisk the rebel, who disapproved of the British Empire, but ended up marrying a big business man and must have lived in some kind of mansion.

Poppy's patience soon waned. Inspections, visits from the rector, children reciting their catechisms, certificates and attendance medals presented ... and all of it difficult to decipher. Absences on a large scale too, with half the school missing because of harvest. But no Freers at all, page after page, until at last Tamarisk Freer received ten lashes for insolence.

Poor Tamarisk! Poppy imagined the raw flesh. Whatever she'd said or done, Poppy was sure she wasn't wrong, just ahead of her time. The Nelson Mandela of Wildwood, taking a stand on principle and being punished for it. Even Ed would think that was cool.

Chapter Six

That night Poppy pulled out the picnic basket and looked for pictures of the adult Tamarisk after the wedding. She wanted to find a grandma for Lanky and Sorrel, older and greyer but still magnifique. She turned page after page but found no such pictures. Poppy thought it was just as well that she was keeping colour footage of the wedding itself in her head, because oddly there was no record of that either. But now, of course, she knew Hebe, recognising her in the black and white shots with her daughters, the woman with the jello-mould hair. Of course Paul Golding must have been holding some kind of little box camera and taking all the pictures. And if he was, then the smiles were really for him, full ones, comfortable, sometimes laughing, always bright-eyed. Paul Golding, the conchie. Sorrel's dad.

Poppy had put the family tree in a drawer by the bed. By torchlight she took another look, trying to memorise the dates like she'd done in school with the Tudors. Finally folding it away, she realised she couldn't sleep, so she ended up sending the same text to Min and Katie: *Gorgeous donkeys and even more gorgeous boy. Staying on. P x* She could picture their faces when they read it.

The next morning she took Lanky breakfast in bed. The fried eggs looked plastic and the beans had become a single meshing dollop, but Lanky said she was the star of the show.

"Which reminds me," she said, "there's a piano at the vicarage so you can keep your practice up. I want to hear you play."

Suddenly Poppy wanted to play that very moment. But there was a quick knock, the turning of a key and a shout from the hall. Natalie had arrived and put on rubber gloves to start the cleaning. And a kind of row.

"I'm not an invalid!" protested Lanky. "And what dirt there is can hang around until I've got my dial back on whiz."

"What dirt there is," countered Natalie cheerfully, "could bury Roman remains!"

"Exactly! Comes in handy when there's a dead donkey!"

It was what Lanky called banter and more good-humoured than most of Poppy's exchanges with Ed. Poppy wondered whether she'd still be friends with Min or Katie in another fifty years. She left Natalie scrubbing out the sink and wandered out to the sanctuary.

Kane was just arriving on his bike. Ed would have scorned it. Bony and neglected, and sadly short of gears, this bike had a chain that looked too brown for its own good.

"Rain scald?" asked Poppy, as he leaned the bike against the fence.

"Ho, ho," said Kane. "Sharp."

"Ouch," she murmured, looking at the contours of the torn saddle, concerned for the small backside lost in his baggy jeans.

"I'll survive."

"Where do you live?" she asked.

"Eddington. Council estate. The people round here probably signed a petition to stop it. There's a sign outside: BEWARE OF PROBLEM FAMILIES."

"Ho, ho," said Poppy.

"Are you going to help with the mucking out today?" he asked, tightening his belt and hitching up his jeans.

"Can do," she said, as if she didn't mind.

"You're all right," he said. "That's my job. Part of the conditions. The point-making." He grinned into the sun. "You can feed the donkeys but remember Cinnabar is half-blind. Don't let her mistake your fingers for carrots."

Poppy noticed he was browner than he'd been when she arrived.

"You're getting a tan," she said.

"So are you," he said, looking at her arms as they reached out to open the gate. "Or is that rain scald?"

She couldn't help smiling. It was the way he said it, trying not to laugh at his own joke even before he'd made it.

"Gotcha, didn't I?"

Oh yes, thought Poppy. He was looking relaxed today. It suited him. As she gave the donkeys their breakfast she compiled a mental list of facts about Kane Bradley, and realised how few she'd discovered. One loved-up mother with a new man and Lol. A council estate in Eddington. A rubbish bike. A father, but who, and where, and how often did Kane see him? Talk of punishment and rehabilitation, but for what? He was almost as mysterious as Sorrel, and she suspected he chose to be.

He set to with the sweeping, his music in his ears. Letting her get on with breakfast could have been trusting or unhelpful, depending on how Poppy looked at it. Misty, the smallest jenny, ignored her, but Jerry was louder than ever when he got a sniff of food, and nudged her stomach impatiently so she had to tell him to behave. George seemed glad to see her, lifting his head as if he didn't seem to realise he just wasn't big enough to rub ears with hers. Joely's undershot jaw didn't stop her giving Louise an affectionate neck-groom. Poppy remembered they were mother and daughter and supposed it was like her own mum brushing her hair when she was smaller, or clipping the fingernails on her right hand when she asked her nicely.

One by one she led them into one of the stables for a pulp of dried sugar beet which Kane had mixed with cabbage. She'd describe it for Min and Katie as rank. *Well* rank. But they seemed hungry enough, most of them. It was odd to think that anybody trying to be generous and feed up a donkey with delicious, protein-packed and vitamin-rich food could kill it. Donkeys survived on rubbish in the wild, a bit like Ed.

Poppy had a list of how much to weigh out for each donkey, but although she was learning their names she couldn't be a hundred percent about all of them.

Having worked through the donkeys she knew, she was forced to confess her confusion to Kane, who was singing along with something under his breath as he swept. He grinned as if to say he'd been waiting for her to need rescuing. It was much quicker with two of them and she paid him back by helping him clear the donkey dung and wet straw.

But there was one donkey left.

Midge was still in isolation and Poppy wasn't supposed to go near her, but while Kane was finishing up in the paddock she sneaked up to the field with a bucket of breakfast and risked opening the gate just enough to put it on the other side. Not that there was much chance of Midge leaving her corner to come and get it.

Kane appeared and slung his grey hoodie across the fence.

"I wouldn't tempt some of the greedy ones," he said, smoothing the sleeve, "but I think it's safe with Midge."

"Do you think we're safe with Midge really?" asked Poppy. "Wasn't it a one-off? You know, a blip?"

"Something snapped, you mean?" said Kane. "Maybe, yeah."

"I snap sometimes," said Poppy, "but mostly privately, on the inside."

"So no one else has to deal with the mess?" asked Kane. "You're left to clear up your own?"

"I suppose," she said, "but you know what it's like with mess. It's easier to leave it."

"That way it can accumulate." He grinned. "Wouldn't work very well round here."

Poppy smiled and wrinkled her nose.

"If it's private and internal, it's not really snapping," Kane said. "I'd call that feeling. I think you're a nice normal girl and you want to know if I snap. And if that's why I'm here on donkey duty, repaying my debt to society." He looked away towards Midge. "You're probing."

"No," she protested.

"I'm nothing like Midge." He paused, and scuffed some dandelions that sprouted by the gate with the tip of his trainer. "Well, we're both a bit scrawny. But she can't do this."

He jumped over, cowboy-style. She was watching him approach Midge with the bucket in his hand when Dan the vet arrived, walking slowly so that a limping Lanky could keep up. With them was a man Poppy's mum would call a silver fox, a gleaming one. Her dad was working towards that particular objective but until he achieved it Poppy reckoned he was piebald.

"This is Ryan," Lanky said. "He's an animal communicator."

Ryan said a low "Hi." He was probably about forty-five but looked as if his hobby was triathlons. His grey hair was tied back but looked a lot shinier and healthier than a donkey tail. He had a nose stud which Poppy mistook at first for a drop of sweat glinting in the sun.

"I think," said Ryan, "that Midge feels a little overcrowded."

"Would you mind, you two?" asked Lanky.

She managed to sit down with her bad leg straight, to watch from the gate. She suggested that Kane could call it a day. Poppy felt disgruntled. Kane shrugged, jumped back over again and said that was fine by him. He fitted his music back into his ears and headed off without a glance. Dan and Ryan made their way towards Midge.

Poppy found a spot where the grass was lush, with nothing to prickle a bare midriff. As she lay down, her ring tone sounded and she clicked it off quickly in case it drove

Midge wild with its solid drum and bass kick-in and saxophone wail. It was Min, wanting to know how she was.

"Hey!" she cried. "Yeah. Turning golden brown. It's really hot."

Min said it sounded as if this boy was hot. Poppy giggled.

"Kind of."

Min wanted more, of course.

"Dunno. Sixteen maybe. Skinny. Short hair, piercings …"

Min asked whether he was a bad boy. Poppy paused.

"He might be."

Suddenly Poppy didn't really want to say any more but Min was asking whether he was a hoodlum like Gary Hylands in Year 9.

"Hoodlum?" mocked Poppy. "Are you sure you don't mean gangster? Well, maybe. I don't know. He's been in trouble …"

Min asked what kind – mugging old ladies, or did she mean drugs?

"He wouldn't mug old ladies! I think he's got a temper, though. Suppose he might do drugs. How would I know? He hasn't offered me any weed!"

Min wanted to know whether he was a posh upper class bad boy with a horse because she'd heard they were the worst with drugs. Poppy laughed.

"As if! He lives on a council estate. And his bike ... well, put it this way: if it was a donkey Lanky would have to think about putting it down!"

What had happened to the sun? Poppy rolled over and there he was. Kane, the grey hoodie over his arm, stood looking down at her. She looked back, her mouth falling open. He reached out a hand and at first she thought he was offering it for her to grab, so he could pull her up. But he was asking for the phone. Demanding, waiting. Dumbly Poppy handed it over.

"Grow up, little girl," he told Min, and clicked it off. Then he handed it back.

"Kane ..." she said, burning.

"You should have said if you wanted me to sort you out. Crack cocaine, best heroin. I hang round the schools at home time."

"I'm sorry, Kane," she begged. There was nothing to say. She'd said it all.

"I'm the one who's sorry," he said, his voice quiet but stiff, and flat, as if he was trying to stop it being something very different. "But you're right about one thing – the temper. You can probably tell."

She could. She could hear it, gusty and wild. He was walking away, without bothering to put the music back into his ears. He kicked the fence as he left the field but if he'd hurt himself he didn't let it show. And she couldn't call after him, not with Dan and Ryan and Midge and Lanky all within hearing distance. She couldn't say anything. And anyway she'd said too much, and all of it stupid and childish, teen brat and mean and completely pathetic.

Poppy started to cry. He'd be gone soon, on the bike. And what would she do when he came back tomorrow? Would he come back tomorrow?

Lanky looked in her direction and shaded her eyes. Poppy composed herself and walked over, slowly and self-consciously.

"Have you upset him?" Lanky guessed. Maybe she'd heard some of it. Poppy nodded, not trusting herself to speak. She looked away to Ryan and Midge who were trying to trust the silence.

"He'll get over it," Lanky said, quick and casual, almost whispering. "It's not the first time." She looked back because Midge was out of the corner.

"See?" said Lanky. Midge was plodding forward, eyeballing the silver fox. "This is pretty amazing stuff. I wish Kane had seen it."

Poppy sat down with her. Dan, who had edged further back towards the gate, raised his eyebrows at them. Poppy wasn't sure anyone should be breathing, never mind speaking.

Then without warning Midge flicked up her neck and opened her jaws. A sawing scrape of a cry throbbed its way up from her chest and out like a carburettor. Her teeth were bared and enormous and her head was on a hinge, backwards and forwards, up and down like a child on a rocking horse out of control. Her legs were flailing too, and she was pivoting around on her new spot, the space Ryan had persuaded her to fill.

Ryan put out his hand, but thought better of it as Midge brought her head down not too far from his fingers. Lanky rose to her feet and pushed the gate open, hobbled in and waited, talking, chirruping, only just out of range of teeth and hooves. Midge stilled, kicked her back legs, then stilled again.

"There, there, all over now, girl," murmured Lanky.

Midge hung her head and kept her eyes low to the ground, but she didn't move. Lanky patted the donkey's neck and stiff, unkempt back.

"Shall Midge and I resume our conversation, Mrs Jones?" asked Ryan.

"Better still," said Lanky, "would you fill that corner of hers with wheelbarrows, the pair of you? You should find plenty lying around."

Ryan didn't argue, but when the two men wheeled the barrows behind her Midge noticed. Her head turned. It tilted and swayed as she leaned in towards the space, her legs starting to follow. She didn't look angry or dangerous, just forlorn, as if she was grieving for something she'd lost. Lanky didn't try to hold her back against her will. As Ryan and Dan moved themselves and the barrows out of the way she slotted herself back into the comfort of her corner and became completely silent. Nothing moved. She was an image, a freeze-frame, her eyes ahead and at rest.

Lanky shifted the bucket so that Midge would scarcely have to move to reach it. Dan and Ryan were through the gate before she'd finished.

"I'll call you," Lanky told Ryan when she joined them.

"She was responding so well," he said.

"I thought so too."

"There are bad memories there. Surfacing them ..."

"May have been too much too soon," finished Lanky.

He made no comment.

"You did what you do," said Lanky. "No blame. She just isn't ready, poor sausage."

"I'd like to try again."

"In good time."

As Poppy watched the two men walking away to the drive she knew she needed to go too. She told Lanky she wouldn't be long and made her way to her temporary bedroom. There she would read her book or play her music, and try to delete. She'd hurt Kane. Or made him despise her, which was worse. Either way he wouldn't bother with her again.

The house smelt flooded with toilet cleaner, like a fake pine forest that made noses drip. Poppy preferred the smell of cake. Natalie had gone, presumably before the drama began, and left a note, so when there was a knock on the door Poppy thought that like Kane she must have come back for something she'd left behind. But it was her father, and Poppy knew she was staring.

"David Golding," she murmured. "Hullo, Dad."

"Darling," he said quietly. He wore his craggy grey work face so his smile was an effort. It had to crack a way through.

"It's not the best of times, Dad," she said, and as he hugged her she wasn't prepared. What was it she felt? Discomfort? Whatever it was, she knew it showed.

"Oh, thanks," he said. "It's lovely to see you too."

"I didn't mean … well, it's a bit dramatic round here."

"Should suit you perfectly," he said, and she pulled an Ed face at his smile.

David said he hadn't got long. Poppy thought he looked out of place for someone who had known this house since before she was born. He sat down, looking tired, so she put the kettle on. He had been to a meeting not far away, he continued, and thought he'd drop in and check on them both.

"Sorry, Dad," said Poppy. "I need the loo."

She almost ran, and when she emerged from the bathroom, telling herself she wasn't nervous and it was her father's fault for being so tense, she found he'd gone outside with his tea. Poppy watched from the window as he hugged Lanky, a little carefully. She couldn't hear what they said, which was odd because Lanky normally spoke loudly enough to address the village end to end. The two of them walked slowly back to the house, close but separate, eyes mainly down. Poppy supposed her father was protecting his polished business shoes.

Poppy made more tea. Lanky didn't want to talk about Midge, the leg or how she was coping.

"Those boys," she told David. "There must be something newsworthy. Dish the dirt."

Poppy's father took a moment to gather it together. But then he admitted there was more information about Nick's girlfriend, who was another volunteer. Normally Poppy would be wide-eyed and inquisitorial like a journalist on the story, establishing the facts, asking about feelings and embellishing with speculation. She only smiled and knew it wasn't convincing. Apparently Ed was still out of step with the household when it came to diet and sleep patterns. Her dad said he was refusing to use the deodorant that had been bought for him.

"His socks put the public at risk," said Poppy. "Health and Safety will come knocking one day."

But she knew she needed to work on her delivery, and besides, her humour had done enough damage today.

The news about her father's work was not so interesting. And there was something about the two of them, facing each other across the table, that made her feel superfluous, a child again. She asked Lanky if she could listen to some of her wild old classical collection. The records were stacked up in torn and bent sleeves in a cabinet in the lounge.

"Don't worry, I'll turn the volume up," she said. "You can get back to your secrets."

When neither of them denied or argued, Poppy considered giving the door a pointed slam but only sighed and knelt down to thumb her way through the snubbed corners. There was no kind of order. She picked a cello concerto by Elgar but it was the saddest thing she'd ever heard and as it swelled she lifted the old needle into silence. Most of which came from the kitchen.

Poppy looked in to find Lanky on the edge of tears and her father's hands closed around hers on the table. When she joined them she almost felt she should cough a warning. They both managed a smile for her, but she thought none of them were very good at acting, least of all her. She barely tried. If they had their secrets, so did she. The music had made her think of Kane and Midge and Sorrel Golding.

"Talk to your dad, Poppy," Lanky told her. "He's got to be going soon."

Lanky left them, gasping as she stretched her bad leg, and hobbled into the lounge to select some sleepy, dreamy Brahms. Poppy wasn't sure she liked being told to talk. She looked at the flowers instead.

"Lanky tells me you want to find out about your ancestors," said David, slowly fingering the rim of his empty mug.

"Yes," she dared, thinking better of denying it.

"If it's your grandmother you mean, we'd like you to leave things alone for now."

"No kidding," said Poppy.

His mouth set. She knew he didn't like it when she was sarcastic.

"But Paul Golding and the conscientious objection are interesting," he added, lightly, moving on and getting up. "I don't know whether you'll find out much."

"I'll try," she said, and he started explaining conscientious objection as if she was Tim. But she let him talk, looking around distractedly and at one point repositioning a stem in the vase. He said he must be going.

At the door she hugged him and wished they could start again. He asked whether she was happy to stay on and she said yes, knowing she sounded anything but. Then he remembered a letter from her mum, which looked slightly mangled when he eased it out from inside his jacket pocket. Lanky waved goodbye from the upstairs window and he opened the car door.

"I love you, Dad!" called Poppy from the doorway, almost tripping over shoes and umbrellas and a stack of newspapers.

David heard. He turned, and his smile was sudden and wide. Then he got into the car with another wave and was gone. It was true, Poppy thought, about those three magic words. And she'd meant them, even though they sounded overblown and childlike as they'd made their way to him.

But weren't they supposed to be a trigger, to act like a hammer on the knee, provoking a response? A reflex would have done. When she tried to hear him echo them back in her head it wasn't the same. She couldn't get the tone of voice quite right, because she couldn't remember the last time he'd said it.

Poppy might have read her mother's letter straight away, but she was afraid it would make her little girly and she needed to think clearly and maturely now. She tucked it under the clock in her bedroom for later. There were things that had to be said.

After she'd made Lanky an omelette she asked where Kane lived. Lanky told her the address after checking the back of an envelope tucked behind the dusty teapot.

"Write him a letter," she said. "It's a dying art and ideal for peacemaking. You can cross out or delete until you get the words just right. No blurting. Or putting your size nines in it the way I do."

Poppy considered.

"Vic and Natalie will drop it in," said Lanky. "They walk Mo before bed."

Vic wasn't Vic really. It was Lanky's joke because he was the vicar. Remembering the way their dog waddled and flumped around the sanctuary, Poppy agreed that she needed serious walking.

She also agreed to the letter even though she hadn't worked out yet exactly what to write.

"Be careful what you say, though, Poppy. Words don't get forgotten or paraphrased when they're on paper."

But Poppy didn't think her dad would forget the last ones she'd given him even though they'd disappeared into sunlight.

After extensive editing and redrafting, the message read: *This idiot is very, very sorry. See you soon. Poppy.* Idiot? Wasn't there a better word? Her mum liked schmuck, but she used it in a playful way and Poppy felt she'd been playful enough already, playing with the idea of Kane as if he was a character in her own drama instead of a life. She hoped the note was enough. It would have to be better than nothing, wouldn't it?

She looked at the creased envelope under the alarm clock as she lay down in bed. Anna Beth's would be a very different letter, because her mother would be missing her. She would read it in the morning. Poppy was afraid she wouldn't sleep, expecting to run through the scenes in her head: Natalie and Vic delivering the note, Kane finding it, reading it, and … what next?

In fact she slept almost straight away, probably even before Mo and her walkers got back from their exercise. But in her dreams the letter was eaten and spat out by a dog that was more like a hound of hell. It turned into Kane, who was choking on her apology until he retched it up in saliva, and then into Midge, who didn't stop shaking. Poppy woke up startled, trying to drop a whip the dream had put into her hand. She took so long to go back to sleep again that she resorted to naming donkeys, not just the real ones a heehaw away, but past or future donkeys that might be called Betsy Trotwood or Scrunchie, Daydream Believer (her mum's favourite song) or Scallywag, Curly or Scrumpy or Dandelion or Rose Garden. Petal or Fuzz or Action Hero. Chilli Pepper or Clementine or plain old Sausage ... or Chips ...

You wouldn't call a donkey Idiot. But Sorry worked, if you said it enough, and it sounded as if it was short for something, a nickname, a friendly one ...

Poppy woke to the certainty that no one had ever used it for Sorrel Golding, because she was too pretty and too proud to be pitied, to hang her head low. But had Sorrel said the word and why? What had she been sorry for?

If Kane wouldn't let her close again, how was she going to tell him she was having ghostly encounters? He'd never have the chance to joke it all away.

Enough now, she told the silence with her eyes closed. No more paranormality. No more imagination of the hyperactive kind. But where were the spirits now that she needed to lay down the law, Lanky-style? The real world felt difficult enough, and in the darkness no one seemed to be listening.

Chapter Seven

Dear Poppy,

I miss you! You knew I'd say that. I've no big jobs on this week so I've decided to get on with the decorating we've been talking about for ages. I'll do your room so if you're fussed about colours, let me know. If not I'll surprise you.

I want to try to explain about your grandma Sorrel – or rather explain why I can't explain. It's not my past, you see, and your dad doesn't want to dig it up. I think he should. I think he should talk to some kind of professional. It's grown bigger and bigger with time instead of smaller and I don't know why. I guess being abandoned by your mother is pretty difficult to live with. His grandparents took care of him, of course, but not for long before they died. Lanky did a great job, but he feels guilty about being dumped on her when she was so young and only just married. He reckons she hadn't wanted kids of her own and finds animals easier to love.

So he doesn't know where Sorrel is or even whether she's still alive. He tried to suppress his feelings and that never holds. The past has gone, it's over, and we have to live in the present and build a future, but the thing about this history is that no one's drawn a line and it keeps on leaking into the now.

You're a step further removed. You can be curious without being overwhelmed by emotion and you want to know. That's fine. You're old enough. Just go gently, and be prepared to keep anything you find out to yourself. I try not to think badly of Sorrel. She was a talented, beautiful girl and everyone loved her. But it's hard not to be angry with her when you look at the damage she did.

I just tell myself that none of us should be judged by the worst thing we've ever done.

Much love,

Mum XXXXXXXXXX

Poppy read it three times between waking and breakfast, and each time she pictured her dad, David Golding, the baby Sorrel didn't want. It made things seem sadder than she'd realised. She remembered the hug and blamed herself for presenting all those angles he'd call teenage, so sharp and jagged when he must have needed soft. She hadn't seen many pictures of him as a boy, but she remembered one in school uniform with a cap and tie, looking very serious, as if his forehead was packed tight with problems. Now she knew it had been.

It wasn't enough. She wanted more; her mother knew she would. But she had to be even more careful than she'd supposed.

A step removed. She was lucky. But it was only one step.

Her mother's letter had reminded her of a rather shorter note. She pushed the duvet back with her feet and showered and dressed as quickly as she could. Lanky's door was shut and she assumed she was still in bed. But through the kitchen window Poppy saw her outside, watering the roses with a plastic can filled from the water butt. Pulling faces with each step and shift of weight, she was focused and determined.

"Ah, Poppy," she called. "Sleep all right?"

Poppy lied. As Lanky limped back indoors she asked her what she wanted for breakfast.

"I've had toast. Can't find anything thanks to Miss Fussypants and her spick and span takeover. She'll be round soon to polish the teaspoons and varnish the door handles. I'll have to change the locks!"

Poppy laughed and noticed the toaster did look rather shiny. It was lighter too, without the ton of black crumbs that used to coat the inside like ash.

"Lanky," she said, "what was your career before the donkeys?"

Lanky sat down on a kitchen chair, stiff and breathing out.

"Not brain surgery or concert piano. Flowers! I had my own shop in Highover. I just wanted to be independent and do as little harm as possible. I might not look like a bloom the way I was supposed to, but they're part of me. People need flowers in their lives."

Poppy agreed. She imagined her dad in the school holidays, helping out with armfuls dripping across the shop floor. He still knew all the names and which cost most.

"Your great grandmother was musical, you know."

This was an unexpected crumb. Poppy tried not to look too eager for more.

"Hebe? Did she sing?"

"Beautifully. And played too. She earned money from performing at one time, before she had babies rather late in life. Settled for Gilbert and Sullivan and church concerts later on. I'm telling you because you love your music. That's all." There was something final in Lanky's tone. She sent a text and started rooting around in a cupboard, refusing Poppy's offer of help.

"As far as my father Paul is concerned," she continued, "Natalie will take you to meet someone who might be able to throw a bit of light on the conscientious objection side of things, but she's nearly eighty and a bit misty at times so don't expect too much. I'd come too if I could ..."

"Who is she?" asked Poppy.

"My father's little sister, back from New Zealand. I neglect her shamelessly – hardly knew her at all before she emigrated – but she's on Saint Natalie's good works list. Kathleen Golding. Far end of the parish, past Eddington."

Eddington. Beware the problem families. Would Kane come today? Poppy told Lanky she'd like to meet Kathleen, and when Natalie arrived in a hippie tie-dyed top with a cheerful smile and bright cerise lipstick it was all arranged. But the donkeys came first.

Kane was expected. He just didn't arrive. So things were slower than usual and Natalie tried his mobile but it seemed to be switched off.

"What did you put in that note, Poppy?" Natalie teased, weighing out food. "I hope you haven't broken his heart."

"I wish," said Poppy, and coloured, but only the donkeys saw and they weren't telling.

It was late morning by the time they were finished. Midge wasn't any hungrier than usual when Dan called by to check her out. Natalie said she was afraid the donkey was going to waste away and it would be another blow for poor Lanky. Poppy felt as if she should be able to communicate with Midge as well as any silver fox who charged for it, just by looking her in the eyes with the kind of love that made you brave, the kind mothers were supposed to give children, full of faith and unconditional. But no one was going to let her near enough to try.

Natalie suggested cycling to Kath Golding's place, which meant Poppy using Lanky's bike. Like its owner, it was sturdy, muddy and not very stylish, but she adjusted to it and got a rhythm going. She could have overtaken Natalie on her flashier silver model, nicknamed Hawkwind, but she let her lead the way. It was hot and she didn't want to sweat too obviously, since Kath Golding lived past Eddington.

Not that she had a plan. Just thoughts that wouldn't go away.

Poppy enjoyed the ride almost as much as Natalie obviously did. But she was conscious all the way of a hidden agenda. She looked out for Kane's estate as soon as the fork sign at the end of a lane directed them to Eddington. There was no sign of him, or of Lol wheeled round by her mother. Not at the old-fashioned, wooden shelter bus stop, or around the row of tatty and rather random shops that included a chippie and a double glazing place with white plastic doors leaning up outside.

Then they were back in rural England again, with well-cut hedges and trim borders, fields on all sides of the narrow road and footpath signs above stiles. Few cars passed, and the lane slipped away at the edges as if nature was nibbling it away. Poppy saw a sparrowhawk hovering over corn, a loner like Midge but unafraid. She was so busy watching it that she almost dived over the handlebars as the wheel angled into a crack that Natalie blamed on snow.

Kathleen Golding lived in sheltered housing and Natalie chatted with the warden first before knocking loudly at Kath's door. It opened eventually and slowly. The small woman invited them in, but it was a few moments before a sudden smile of recognition loosened and smoothed her face. She reached slowly down to a drawer and pulled out a stiff linen apron covered with birds and flowers, neatly folded and unworn. This she tied on, explaining the need to smarten herself up. Inside it, her slight frame was encased in home knitting that was as dull and flat as the carpet. Her face was oval and her pale blue eyes enlarged by black-framed glasses. Natalie made the introductions, arm round Poppy. She referred to her as Lanky's great niece.

"Baby David's girl? Sorrel's David?"

Kath Golding took off her glasses to wipe one eye, leaving it reddened. Poppy saw how paper-thin the skin lay, grey as a bruise and dipping underneath. She invited them to sit down but the black cat in the armchair was disinclined to move until she flapped her fingers. It sprang off, rubbed against Poppy's legs and darted out to a shared lawn, mown like a tennis court, where two elderly women were playing croquet.

Kath made tea in her best cups, balancing ginger biscuits on the saucers. Poppy, who was hungry, was disappointed to find hers soft, its flavour faded to peppery card. Natalie was a revelation. She asked, complimented, remembered, informed and noticed. Kath Golding loved her. Poppy wondered whether she had all this stuff stored away in some kind of file on her computer. But what interested Poppy was how much Kath had stored away herself, and whether she could trust it.

"Poppy would like to know about your brother's tribunal, Kath."

"I was there."

"Oh, really? That must have been emotional for you? But you would have been very young."

"We were evacuees. We came up from the smoke. They separated us but he found me and persuaded, begged … until they put us together again. He had a very quiet voice, but there was something about him even then … He grew into a man while we were here, you see. He fell in love and got married to a lady."

She emphasised the last word like an infant, looking at Poppy.

"A real lady, called Hebe Madison. She sang like an angel. Mother wouldn't let me go to the wedding because people in the village disapproved. She thought we'd be pelted with abuse instead of confetti."

"He was a conscientious objector?" prompted Natalie.

"Hebe was proud of him but she was the only one. Well, I was proud of him too. He was my big brother, you see. I don't agree with pacifism. But he was always very kind to me."

"Where was the tribunal held, Kath?"

"Like a court, my mother said, as if he was a criminal. Some of the neighbours in Hackney got wind somehow and sent nasty notes. 1943, it was. Terrible rain."

"Do you remember the tribunal?" persisted Natalie. Poppy just watched her in admiration.

"I was too young to go. Twelve, or eleven. But I know she was there. Hebe Madison, very elegant she was. It was just before the wedding. Or just after ..." She lowered her voice and leaned forward a little. "Some people said she only saved him so she could keep him there in her bed. Even my mother said it was unnatural, her being so much older." Kath sat back again, upright now. "I thought it was a fine thing, what she did. And she was fine too, very fine."

"Saved him?" Poppy couldn't let that go. "How did she save him?"

Kath Golding stared at her as if she wasn't sure where she had come from.

"With her love," she said, as if it was both obvious and momentous.

Then she started to apologise for the mess and not making them any tea, and went out to the kitchen to make more. They heard her talking about shoes and hats and thunderstorms, but she was looking out of the window and they weren't sure they were meant to hear.

"I'm not sure she knows much hard fact," Natalie whispered. "I'm sorry, Poppy. Why don't you get some air and I'll see what else I can find out. It's pretty out that way. There's a footpath ..." She gave directions. Poppy wasn't sorry to go. The flat was stuffy and she didn't like to think of

Sorrel Golding getting older, with bruised, papery skin under leaking eyes.

Outside the flats Poppy stood uncertain as the idea took hold. Eddington wasn't more than a few minutes' ride back. It had air, even if Natalie wouldn't call the place pretty. Poppy pedalled fast, the wind cooling her face, until she reached the bus shelter and the row of shops.

A woman was bending over a buggy handing a toddler an ice cream. Poppy leaned her bike against the back of the shelter and took a chance.

"Excuse me," she said. "I'm looking for the Bradley family. They live on the estate but I don't know the number."

"Sorry, I can't help you, love."

As Poppy thanked her, a man in baggy shorts stepped out of the newsagent's with a paper.

"Number twenty-three," he said. "Karen Bradley married my girlfriend's ex."

Poppy wasn't sure what to say to that except "Thank you." The estate wasn't hard to find. She wheeled her bike beside her and followed the shorts. The estate was bigger than she expected, and neater too. No warning signs. Some kids were kicking a ball around in a grassy space, and there was a playground which was busy with mothers and small children. No Lol, though. She checked.

Numbers 16 – 31. Suddenly Poppy couldn't do it, whatever it was she'd intended to do. Knock on the door, she supposed. And say what? He'd think she was a stalker, obsessed with him. How stupid could she be?

She turned away and climbed on the bike. She was beginning to panic that she'd forgotten the way back to Kath

Golding's village when she saw him. Kane was sitting waiting for the bus in the shelter, his face shadowed, his legs stretched out long in his bleached, holey jeans. His head was lowered to his phone. He might not even see her if she just rode on. So now that she'd found him she kept her eyes ahead and tried to pick up speed.

"Hey!" he called.

Poppy stopped, pulled over onto the pavement, wheeled back and dismounted. She leaned the bike against the shelter and half-smiled.

"What are you doing?" he asked.

"Bike ride." She paused, trying to read him. "You didn't come to the sanctuary."

"I told Lanky I wouldn't be in till the afternoon."

"Oh."

Lanky must have forgotten. So he wasn't ill, or sulking. Poppy managed a real smile.

"Bike's had an accident. Someone kicked it to death. Wasn't you, was it? You weren't a big fan." He grinned. "I fell off." He showed her the grazes on his hands and elbows.

"Ouch," she said.

"I got your apology. I see you've got the vicar running errands."

She waited, but he looked away. She wished the bus would come. She hoped it wouldn't.

"Forget the song. Sorry isn't the hardest word. It's easy. Two syllables, out of the mouth, light as air," he said. "But they don't change anything."

She nearly said it again, automatically. "I know," she said instead.

"Good."

She thought he wanted her to sweat like this. He'd had his punishment, maybe was still serving his sentence, whatever it was for. This was hers and it was what she deserved. She accepted it in the pause and the face he didn't offer. Then he put his hands in his pockets.

"There are some flats round here that used to be Robert Madison's big old house."

"What? Where Tamarisk lived, before she left him?"

"Yeah."

"How do you know?"

"I do time at the estate agent's. That's where I was this morning. There's what they call a luxury apartment up for sale. They kept the outside as close as possible to the old Victorian front, but it was converted into flats years ago. The history's a selling point, see, because Madison was the big noise of the area. A real fat cat."

He had been doing his own research. So he'd forgiven her and she wanted to thank him. But she wished he'd trust her. From the back pocket of his jeans he produced the estate agent's details. She took the sheet and thanked him.

"'s nothing," he said. "It's boring there. I'd rather muck out donkeys."

He stood up. The bus was slowing to a stop.

"There's probably nothing to see," he added, hand raised.

She climbed on her bike and pedalled off because she told herself she could hardly stand and watch him get on the bus and disappear. Checking her watch, she decided she had time to find the flats if she could do it quickly. There were directions on the sheet, from The Coppice pub which was next to the double glazing place. She followed them and inside five minutes was looking up at her great, great grandmother's married home.

She could see how impressive it must have been. The household must have been run by servants and had bells below stairs to summon them. Poppy wandered around the side, hoping for a better view of the back of the flats, which was where the garden would have rolled down towards the fields. She imagined it with borders and paths, fountains and arbours and blossom. Now the flats sat in the middle of a square of green like a larger version of the felt you could buy in art shops. It was as if the large, shiny pots sprouting plants were holding down the edges to stop them flapping. They were just a finishing touch. It wasn't homely or even very alive.

There were newer houses where the old garden used to be. Like seaside bed and breakfast places, terraced and no longer smart, they looked out of time and place. They had the kind of gardens her dad would scoff at, and complain there was *no room to swing a cat,* as if anyone but a psycho would do that. With nothing to see of Robert Madison's mansion on account of the wall around it, Poppy walked on down a fenced-in track at the back of it, a kind of footpath where the trees hung over and roots tried to burst through underneath. There were gaps where the wooden panels had bent apart or been cracked by branches. Finding a large one she peered through it into one of the gardens where cats couldn't be swung to anyone's satisfaction, imagining one such moggy hurled over hedges and washing lines until it lifted off into space.

The garden was yellow-grey with paving, and rectangles of bleached stones where coloured grasses sprang fashionably. It was impossible to imagine the acres the Madison gardener had kept in order, or Tamarisk on her knees to weed the rose beds in full layered skirts. If there had been swings, or a vegetable plot for the children to seed, or a play house of the kind Queen Victoria's princes and princesses had enjoyed on the Isle of Wight, no one would have guessed. Poppy supposed the evidence must be there, deep in the soil somewhere, but there was nothing to see and nothing much to feel except disappointment.

But something was stirring like wind. Poppy knew at once. She felt excitement but it was the sharp, nervous kind that caught in her chest. Anticipation. It was what she'd come here for and it was no good squealing a protest inside. And here they were, delivery on cue. Like a chain of folded paper figures, a woman and her three daughters stretched out in a swirling swelling line of fabric and lace and flowing hair. The two smallest were almost identical, stumbling stumpy in loose cotton dresses, holding white bonnets to their heads against the wind. The other was longer and thinner, her hair ribboned and curled. She was in the middle, connecting them with one hand each. Tugged by a billowing gust and their own momentum, they ran from the sloping lawn, their laughter and squeals carried with them down towards the woods where the garden finally ended.

Poppy named them: Tamarisk, with Hebe aged four perhaps, and Camellia and Celandine, too short for their names, too small to be more than rounded buds. But weren't there more? Where were the boys to continue Robert Madison's business and the family name?

In no more than moments they were gone again, as if they had slipped on down into the woods, stiffened and rooted, stretching out branches instead of lace-cuffed arms. Poppy turned back towards their old home, but with no way of getting closer or seeing over the wall, was about to return to the bike that she'd propped against it.

It was the cello that stopped her. The sound was faint at first, but the volume surged like a dial spun. It was playing something familiar, something tragic and tender. Bach. Poppy loved Bach. She strained to listen against a lawnmower that jerked into roaring life opposite. But somehow the music wasn't buried. As she tried to focus, it swelled and ached and filled her head. It expelled the motor's whine, the voices, a dog barking at a bee and a car with a radio's dance beat, shrinking them to background until all that was left was the cello, lifting, soaring, live. And at eye level the wall that kept her from the flat was breaking up without a hammer, without dust or debris, as if it no longer existed – until through young, thin branches she saw the upstairs window, open and pouring the music out into sunshine. Clearly now she saw the shape of Hebe Madison embracing the cello, her hair swaying with the strike and drag of the bow across the strings, her head back as the note held. Like Poppy's breath.

The window filled with black as a man grabbed the bow and beat it across the back of Hebe's head, brought it down on her shoulder and then, as she cowered, against her stooped back. The instrument that thudded and clanged to the floor trailed into silence, but the rhythm had begun and it did not stop as Robert Madison hit his daughter Hebe again and again. There was a snap and a jagged edge as the thin wood clattered to the floor in a final beat.

"No!" cried Poppy. It was beyond anything she might have dreamed. And she didn't want it. She shut her eyes. "Leave her alone!"

The words were in her head, but came from Tamarisk's mouth. The blackness made way for the fullness of skirts and a swathe of colour. Tamarisk held Hebe and the quietness throbbed.

It's over now, over for good.

It was Tamarisk's voice, the last line of the episode. Like a curtain at the end of a scene the wall dropped in place. And another voice, young and familiar, fell like blossom, the words scattering around her:

It was twenty years before I played again.

The lawnmower rose to a throttling drone. A bee lifted murmuring from nectar. Poppy ran to her bike, slung herself on and rode off, wobblier than usual, as the Bach echoed back into her head. Through it pushed a whisper: *Sorrel.* Sorrel again.

When she braked outside Kath Golding's place her cheeks were hot, her forehead damp. On her neck where the hair trickled, the skin burned as if it had trapped the sun. Poppy felt swamped, overwhelmed, like a vase that was suddenly overfull but refusing to free the flowers.

"Please," she murmured outside the flats. "No more. No more now. I know enough. Obsession over. Satisfied. Whatever you want, leave me alone."

But she heard the word again. The name. It wasn't going to end because Sorrel wasn't where she belonged. And she wouldn't see Sorrel wherever she looked for her, because Sorrel was alive. Alive and in pain. She must be. That was what it meant. Tamarisk and Hebe who loved her couldn't rest while she was out there somewhere, cut off from her family and crying. Poppy was sure Sorrel Golding had cried more than anyone should.

Natalie had been looking out for her. Seeing her face at the window, Poppy waved, sheepish now. She went in as beckoned to say goodbye to Kath, who embraced her unexpectedly. The door closed slowly behind them.

"Where were you?" asked Natalie. "I tried your phone."

"Sorry. I got a bit lost. I think it needs charging." So casual. Poppy astonished herself.

Natalie gave her that look that said *teenagers* and suppressed a sigh. They started off, and Poppy was glad not to talk as Natalie pedalled ahead, casting back observations about wildlife, some of which blew away before Poppy could decipher them. The ride seemed long and the breeze tugged hard. As they approached the sanctuary Natalie stopped suddenly, so that Poppy had to brake too.

"Kath thinks her brother's tribunal took place in the town hall in Highover. There must be records if you're interested. He was always cleverer than her, she said, and wrote poetry. She thinks the marriage was very happy in spite of the hate campaign, which ran its course. Love is stronger, that's what she believes."

Poppy felt her smile grow.

"I hope so," she said, believing it too.

"Have you been visiting Kane Bradley?" asked Natalie, eyes narrowing.

"I bumped into him."

"Really? That was nice for you."

It struck Poppy as outrageous that Natalie was more inclined to believe an eighty-year-old who contradicted herself than a teenager.

"I did!" she retorted.

"Warning, Poppy. Lanky likes Kane. So do I. He's had some tough breaks and he's a good lad at heart. But if she thinks you're mooning around besotted with him, sneaking off to see him secretly ..."

"I'm not!"

"She'll send you packing. She's seen it before: bad influence, bad choices, love gone wrong, heartbreak, all that."

"Sorrel?"

"No comment, Poppy, as they say."

Natalie cycled up Lanky's drive. Poppy got off and pushed. She felt very tired, and not sure whether to cheer because Hebe was happy with Paul Golding, or cry for Sorrel and all the pain that seemed to hang around her, even now that she was just a word.

Without looking for Kane, she went upstairs for a shower. Natalie wouldn't blab. Vicar's wives were like doctors, weren't they, sworn to confidentiality? Poppy would wash her hair, put on something clean and cool and wander casually in his direction. She had a few things to tell him.

The facts were stacking up. But she'd have to be less than open about her sources. Insight, she could call it, beyond the data. And she knew that there was more to see, deeper in.

No choice and no point in resisting. Get through the nightmares, she told herself, and see it through to the end.

Chapter Eight

Maybe it was because he had started late that day, but Kane seemed in no hurry to go home. And Poppy was in no hurry for supper. She told him how Robert Madison had hit Hebe, and how she hadn't played again for twenty years after that.

"Until Sorrel was born!" she realised, doing the maths.

"Who told you this?" asked Kane, nail-splitting and threading straw as he lay sideways on grass, propped up by an elbow. "The bricks or the trees?"

"Why are you doing time at the estate agent's?" she countered, wondering what she'd do if he told her and she had to do the same. But he acted as if he hadn't heard.

"Have you been on one of those ancestry websites?" he guessed, sitting up.

"Maybe," she said, grabbing three strands of straw to find out whether she could have earned a small living plaiting them, like Tamarisk's poorer classmates might have done. It took concentration, which was fine. A distraction, and he was impressed.

"The Internet won't tell you stuff like that," he scoffed, as if cross at his own gullibility. "Who'd know? Only the family."

"Tell-tale servants, I suppose," she said airily, but she knew he wasn't convinced. "People tell secrets like that in diaries."

"Don't tell me you found one buried in the garden?"

"I'm not telling you anything. You're guessing wildly."

"You're maddening," he said.

"Then that makes you mad," she smiled, and had to look away because she didn't want him to see how much she'd amused herself. "I wonder whether Robert Madison was crazed!" she cried, remembering with a shudder inside. "It's not normal behaviour, is it, beating your daughter in a rage with a cello bow?"

Kane looked thoughtful. He said he wouldn't like to define normal behaviour and wasn't sure either of them were very good at it. Then he opened his mouth and lifted his finger. It was funny: a cartoon Eureka moment. She waited, her own mouth open too.

"What year was this?"

"Early nineteen twenties?" suggested Poppy.

"Post-traumatic stress disorder! Shell shock, from the trenches."

It was possible. She nodded, but told him it was no excuse.

"Maybe not. There's such a thing as mitigation. But you're not the judge and jury."

There was something in his voice that made her flinch. Poppy wondered what he knew about judges and juries. Had there been mitigation for him, or did he mean there should have been, but no one cared? She remembered something her mother had said in her letter, about being remembered for the worst thing you'd ever done. She wanted to tell Kane that, but she didn't dare. She didn't know what he'd done and he didn't want her to. But she was sure it wasn't in the same league as Robert Madison, with or without the trenches.

Natalie yelled her name and Poppy hoped Kane wasn't relieved. He didn't say goodbye as he walked away, but he did turn and give her a raised hand, not tilting like the Queen's in her carriage but spread, as if inviting Lol to count. Poppy took a look at Midge on her way back to the house, and found her lying down, looking tired. Or peaceful, perhaps. She'd had a Bach flower remedy that morning and been calm since.

"See you tomorrow, girl," she called, keeping her voice soft and low, and hurried in case the food was on the table. Natalie had gone and the kitchen smelt delicious.

"I'd have invited Kane for supper," said Lanky, as she kicked off her boots, "if you hadn't been here."

"Because I'm too beautiful?" smiled Poppy, washing her hands at the sink, and smelling the oranges in the spinach salad.

"Beauty's not a joke," stated Lanky, and served up.

A little later, as Poppy lay on the sofa, reading to the end of her book at an emotional pace and wiping tears, a text came through.

You might want to check out the churchyard. Go right and up after Fat Cat.

Kane had been investigating again on his way home. She smiled. He'd been thinking about her. Well, about her ancestors anyway.

She waited until Lanky was on the phone, then called up that she'd only be a few minutes and closed the back door quietly behind her. Soon she was back at her great, great grandfather's gravestone. The summer light began to dull and she buttoned up her cardigan as the wind found the bare skin above her jeans. Right and up, she remembered, wondering why boys tried to make three words do. The grass tufted around a flat, square plaque not much bigger than a handkerchief, its corners lost. Two cherubs, fat-cheeked in two senses, sat like tiny dolls at one end, one with its small nose chipped away.

JOHN ERNEST MADISON, 22 months, AND ARTHUR GEORGE MADISON, 10 months, died January13th and 15th 1914.

Poppy could imagine the joint funeral, the two tiny coffins, Robert stiff and black as his own tomb and Tamarisk crying behind a veil. And Hebe by her side, escaping or at any rate surviving whatever had killed her brothers. Typhoid? Smallpox? No vaccinations then, just lots of deaths like these. Poor Tamarisk. Poor Robert, who had no more boys but only flower girls who couldn't love him because he didn't deserve to be loved.

No ghosts. No real world drifts into something else, no torn edges or images thinning. Just eyes wide open investigation. Another mystery solved.

Poppy ran back, checking her watch, determined to make sure that Lanky couldn't suspect her of sneaking off for other reasons more intimately connected with Kane. As she arrived at the back door she found her great aunt waiting for her with her boots on.

"Something's up," she said. "I can feel it."

Poppy hoped she didn't look guilty. After all, she hadn't really done anything.

"Come up with me," Lanky continued, and they walked arm in arm. "There's something in the air, and I don't mean the usual smells."

Opening the gate under the CCTV cameras, Poppy understood what she meant. It wasn't noisy exactly. In fact, she'd heard Jerry create more volume on his own. Even Pinball Wizard addressing an itchy bottom could be a louder and more disturbing business. If there was a thickness of surface noise it was largely hooves shuffling and milling. Very few of the donkeys around the stable area were still, and heads were lifted, alert, turning even before the two of them walked in to be greeted and nudged in the usual way. Which wasn't quite usual. Something was different. At first she wondered whether it was excitement, and for some reason they were stirred up and unable to settle like children expecting Father Christmas. But that wasn't it. Poppy had the feeling they were being told something they needed to understand, and it wasn't exciting. It felt more like distress.

"All right," muttered Lanky. "Someone's in trouble."

"Is it Midge?" asked Poppy fearfully, but she knew George was the oldest of them all.

They made their way through the crowd up into the field where the few Lanky called the twilight donkeys were still enjoying the grass before joining the rest overnight. Freda almost cantered towards them, snorting and throwing back her head, a cloud of flies swarming. Other crowds twisted around at head height, massing black, so that Poppy wished she was a donkey and could dip her head and nudge her way through. Lanky was breathing heavily and leaning harder with one hand on her arm. She spoke to Freda, who slowed and quietened, but attached herself to them like an insecure child at playtime.

It wasn't Midge. She was still in position, still separate, still barely moving. But as they approached she stretched her neck to incline her head towards the lean-to.

Lanky and Poppy moved across towards it as unseen hooves stroked a slow rhythm against one wall inside. A tail hung limp and scrawny from an ample backside that swayed just a little. Ben's ears tilted from one side to the other. He blocked what was left of the light as they looked into the wood and iron shelter. And between his shifting legs Poppy saw a dark shape on the floor.

"Mary?"

His late-life love lay motionless behind him. Poppy hadn't seen a dead donkey before but she didn't need to ask. This wasn't resting or sleeping. She was gone, emptied. And what was left was just a husk, its warmth seeping away into the evening air.

Lanky didn't speak. Her mouth set grim, she laid her free hand on Ben's back and let it edge along, barely ruffling, slow and firm. Poppy stood, one arm still linked, as if the body's stiffness held her tight and drew her own heat away. In her head she heard Kane's voice: *Poppy, you're spending too much time in the company of the dead.* As if he knew the truth of it. As if he had any idea.

"We're going now, Ben," Lanky told him, quiet but clear. "We'll let you mourn. Stay with her as long as you want."

Poppy was crying against her will. Lanky didn't seem to notice. She was holding herself braced. Reaching the gate she left it open.

"In case they want to pay their respects," she said, and Joely and Misty moved at once, through the gap, ambling up onto the field. Louise, Oscar and Stardust followed.

"How do they know?" asked Poppy, watching over her shoulder as they left them behind.

"You could say they want grass or freedom," said Lanky. "You could call them sheep, no brain between them, following any lead."

"But you think they're off to the funeral?"

"They sense it. I'm sure. Of course it could be an announcement as such. After all, they're built to communicate across valleys with those inbuilt loudspeakers of theirs. But I think it's deeper than sound. How many times a day do you communicate without words?"

"So you have to leave her there a while?"

"If we moved her too soon they'd be traumatised. Especially Ben. Poor Ben. He'll need a new routine without her in it."

Lanky said that normally she'd leave the body alone for an hour or two but in this case, seeing as it would be getting dark by then, Mary could stay till morning. She texted Dan and put the kettle on.

"How do people cope in war," asked Poppy, "when everyone keeps dying?"

She'd seen the streets of Iraq, Afghanistan, Gaza. It was horrible; she couldn't imagine living that way, under threat.

"I was born seven years after the war ended," Lanky told her, "but for the adults who'd been through it, it hung around like a ghost at the party."

Poppy let the words settle and didn't dare touch them. She'd only received, absorbed, hoped for more. But the ghost word didn't go away. Hearing it out loud made it scary.

She rang her mother. They had a talk, a nice one, ignoring the content of the letter. Her dad sent her love. Lying awake, too clouded for sleep, she heard the word again, and realised she'd been fending it off for a long time with other words like imagination, but mainly, like the donkeys, by avoiding words at all. She didn't want to think through an explanation because there wasn't one, not one that would make any sense. Tamarisk and Hebe seemed to her more real than dreams but belonging to the same kind of inner world that touched the outside. A kind of intersection. And that wasn't scary at all, nowhere near as scary as war and global warming and the kind of anger that broke people apart.

Then in the morning she overslept. By the time she woke, Lanky and Natalie, and Dan and the money man had removed Mary and made breakfast for the mourners. The air was cool and fresh after overnight rain, and the donkeys smelt different somehow. Poppy hadn't registered that it was Sunday until she heard the bells from the big church in the town. Natalie asked her if she wanted to go to the ten o'clock service but admitted there'd be no clapping or gospel choir. Poppy said she'd rather think outside. Kane didn't come on Sundays and the village shut down in a way Poppy wasn't used to at home.

She could see that she'd have to rely on the donkeys for company.

She was lying on the grass, reading with music through her ears, when her mother arrived with Tim and she burst into tears.

"Are you okay, honey?"

"Mmm," said Poppy. "It's just the shock."

Anna Beth smelt flowery as they hugged. Tim screwed his cheeks up to his eyes and stared at her as if girls were weird. He didn't bother to say hullo, even though Poppy recovered from her embarrassment, remembered how much older and cleverer than him she was, and asked him about his daredevil action camp.

"Cool," he said quickly, as if she'd asked about his toast or socks.

Lanky took him to meet the gang as she called them, and he became more animated straight away.

"He's exhausted after the camp," her mum explained. "I don't think he got any sleep at all. Or washed. His kitbag could have walked back from Devon."

"Why didn't Dad come?" Poppy asked suddenly, missing him and the chance to be less prickly.

"He's taking Ed to cricket. His idea, not Ed's. Sleeping's the most competitive thing Ed can manage at the moment. He broke his own record this week when he surfaced at 1:15."

Her mother asked Poppy a lot of questions and she was conscious that she wasn't giving the fullest of answers. But she knew her mother felt loved. They walked slowly together up to the field. It had been a while since they'd done the arm in arm thing, but Poppy didn't really want to let go.

When they reached the top, Ben was there, pretty much as he always had been, leaning in towards Mary day after day as if he couldn't quite catch what she said. Except that he was closer to the shed, and the nearest head tilted towards him, ears pricked, belonged to Midge. She wasn't out of her corner, not fully. Her back legs were still inside her usual space. But the rest of her had crossed the line in her head, the one that seemed to barricade her in. Her head was down, as if she needed to keep her eyes firmly on the grass below, but her ears were only a few metres from Ben's. They were both equally silent and no eye contact was made. But Lanky reckoned they had reached an understanding.

"She's come out of herself," she murmured as they left them. "That's compassion for you."

After they'd drunk a pot of tea Lanky suggested a walk, just a short one, to keep her leg from seizing up. She kept Tim with her for support, though, and asked his opinions on English football and razzamatazz cricket, and how long it would be before Formula One used hydrogen cell cars. She told him she rather fancied bungee jumping, paragliding and that sport that involved leaping from one rooftop to another, and Anna Beth told them to stop egging each other on. They were both reckless enough. Their conversation was interrupted by a heron that perched above the stream just until they had wandered almost close enough to admire in detail, only to lift off and land again a few metres further along. It was like a game, Lanky said, and no doubt who made the rules.

Meanwhile Poppy told her mum a few snippets, keeping her voice low underneath Lanky's big, deep, chat show questions. She missed out the cello bow. Being beaten was bad enough, and she whispered that part.

"Leaving like that, in those days," her mother said, "was such a huge deal, almost unknown. Tamarisk was one strong woman. I suppose she had to go abroad to make sure he never found her. But I wonder how they managed for money."

Now that the heron had finally tired of toying with them and flown off, Lanky and Tim had stopped a few paces ahead, watching out for the kingfisher often seen on the far bank. Tim was using Lanky's binoculars and each "Cool" was higher-pitched than the last, less of a reflex. The water was mossy green but the light that skimmed it was growing golden.

Lanky looked back as Poppy and her mum closed the gap.

"Tamarisk took a little money, just what she'd had when she married, enough for a few months' rent. She made the girls' clothes and did sewing for other people too, repairs and alterations and outfits children could play in. And of course she had her music, not just playing in bars but teaching too."

Poppy felt a surge of something: excitement and relief. Hebe had told her this. The link wasn't severed after all. And she imagined the paper chain of cotton and windswept hair in the garden, and Lanky reaching out, trying to hold on through time.

"She must have been quite poor, though, after the comfort of being Mrs Madison," said Anna Beth.

"Easier to have dropped arsenic in Robert's tea," said Lanky, deadpan. "But my mother told me that before too long Tamarisk was able to rent the café and serve English teas.

136

Young Hebe helped to serve the customers, with a little frilly white apron, and sometimes the regulars brought ribbons for her hair." Lanky paused. "I should make some scones," she murmured thoughtfully.

"Now?" asked Tim.

Their mother gave him a *behave* signal but Lanky didn't seem to have heard. She squinted into the sunlight at Poppy.

"Sorry to keep you waiting for that. I didn't mean to. Not all the doors are closed, you see, but I almost forget what's behind some of them. And it's only what I remember of what she remembered. It's a flim-flam kind of truth and it can't really have glowed the way it does now."

Tim pointed to something that turned out to be a blue plastic bag. Before anyone could stop him he waded in to retrieve it proudly. The water was only up to his waist but Lanky told him not to drink any because of the rats and he hurried back rather quickly.

Back at the sanctuary, they checked out the donkeys again.

"You'd think they hadn't moved, either of them," said her mum when they found Midge and Ben posed for the same picture. Only the shadows were in different places.

"Midge has taken another step out of her corner," said Poppy.

Lanky smiled.

"Another shuffle, maybe."

Anna Beth couldn't believe it was Midge that bit her. Lanky assured her, as they headed back to the house for more tea, that she would be a hundred percent in a couple of days.

"Poppy's been a rock," she said. "An angel. A combination of the two! But I shan't be leaning on her, literally or metaphorically, much longer. In fact, if you've had enough of donkey dung and housework …"

"Well, if you're sure," said Poppy's mum, "we thought we'd take her back with us if you really can manage now. After all, it's been a lot longer than we intended."

"Oh …" It was more of a noise than a word and ended like a whimper. "No!"

Poppy heard with her mother's ears and wanted it back to try again. But she'd already pulled away, leaving her smarting as if she'd slapped her across the face. How could they understand? She couldn't leave now! Lanky, who was opening the back door, turned to stare intently, her forehead creased.

"Don't I get any say?" Poppy demanded, roughing when she wanted to smooth. "Am I just some kind of package or something?"

"Whoah! Don't you want to come home?" asked Tim.

"Don't be stupid! It's not that …" Poppy didn't know how to finish. "It's just … I need to stay a few more days." She appealed to the doorway, hoping it wasn't too late to be reasonable. "If it's not too much trouble, Lanky."

Lanky raised a finger and opened her mouth wide on all her fillings.

"Ah! It's the concert, isn't it?"

Poppy stared.

"I've got tickets for a recital in town. Chopin? Definitely Schumann. It's a concert pianist from Moscow who happens to be staying locally with his grandmother, who's best friends with my farrier's neighbour. I promised Poppy I'd get her backstage, so to speak. He's a bit of a dreamboat, a Johnny Depp lookalike." She winked at Poppy. "It's on Wednesday. Shall I drive her back on Thursday afternoon? Can you spare her that long?"

Poppy had forgotten how unbelievably amazing Lanky could be.

After the car had driven off, Lanky shut the door and put her hands on her not very obvious hips.

"Thank you, Lanky!" cried Poppy, and kissed her cheek.

"I don't usually tell such bald-faced lies," said Lanky, "or hairy ones either for that matter. I'm not proud of myself. I'd like you to tell me it's not about Kane Bradley. And I'd like that to be the truth."

Poppy opened her mouth. It seemed important to be precise.

"I like him," she said. "But it's more than that. I'd need to stay even if he wasn't around. It's more about them than him …"

"The flower girls."

"Yes," said Poppy, glancing in the mirror, "because I'm one of them."

She saw herself, flushed, any morning make-up worn away by sun and air, her hair streaked with natural blonde highlights, splashing out wildly from a Catherine wheel of a knot, her eyes full of feelings she couldn't have listed, not comprehensively. Behind her was Lanky, bigger, browner and more angular, with eyes equally full and fixed on her. For a moment they both faced the mirror and the two heads, framed.

"You are," said Lanky, "and that's the trouble."

She moved quickly for an invalid, and Poppy knew as she took the stairs at some speed that she didn't want to explain.

Chapter Nine

Poppy was woken early next morning by baking trays, rolling pins and mixing bowls clattering out of a cupboard, and found her great aunt knocking flour from her hair. Lanky must have spent a busy evening on the phone and email, because after apologising for the behaviour of her kitchen equipment she announced a whole series of proposals. And in a way a schedule was reassuring because from the moment Poppy woke she felt muted and heightened at the same time, as if she might cry at an ascending violin or a lit blue sky. As if control might be lost.

But it was a tiring way to start a Monday, especially at five to six, and the list was delivered one item after another like news headlines. And all followed on from the big one: GIRL BEHAVING BADLY. Lanky made it very clear that she never wanted to see or hear her hurt her *poor dear mother* like that again.

"Didn't you ever hurt Hebe without meaning to?" Poppy ventured.

"Yes, of course, so I know what I'm talking about. There's no excuse for hurting those who love you best. You wouldn't forgive it if it was done to you."

Poppy couldn't argue with that. She submitted to the schedule.

Vic and Natalie had invited them to dinner that evening.

There was a toddlers' club at the church hall and Natalie had asked Poppy to help out with the singing as their pianist was on holiday.

Things had to be sorted for a memorial service in Mary's honour.

And Lanky was baking scones straight away, for breakfast. She hoped her mother was watching over her.

"There's also, in fact, a concert at the town hall," Lanky told her, "and as Vic is going into Highover today he'll get us tickets. It's tomorrow and the pianist comes from Hampstead, but the Schumann part was right. I think I must have seen a poster."

Poppy was pleased, although Lanky warned her to forget all thoughts of Johnny Depp.

"Can I go to Highover with Vic?" she asked, bending down to find the butter in the fridge.

Lanky's reaction was delayed, as if she wondered whether she should be suspicious.

"I suppose you haven't been into town. It's not Manchester, mind, but I dare say …"

"I need some tights to wear for the concert. Purple, maybe."

"Ah."

Something made Poppy add the rest.

"And the town hall is where the tribunals took place."

"Aha."

Lanky said she'd ring Vic in an hour if he hadn't already jogged past in his headband by then.

"Does he run?" asked Poppy, impressed.

"No," said Lanky, rubbing in the butter, "he jogs. If you haven't caught sight of him yet, you've missed a treat. Or had a lucky escape."

As it happened, Poppy's first sight of Vic was less than twenty minutes later, while the kitchen grew warm and fragrant with baking. As the heat swelled up the stairs she opened the bedroom window and found a man below. His white hair sprang out from underneath a red towelling headband, a grey vest hung loose around a scrawny chest and two knobbly bruised knees were skimmed by baggy shorts. He must have heard the catch open in the morning quietness because he looked up and waved cheerily. Poppy grinned. On the back of his vest he had the Obama slogan YES WE CAN.

"Go, Vic!" she called, forgetting how early it was and that Vic was not actually his name, but he gave her the thumbs up anyway.

Lanky managed to hand him a warm scone as he passed by again not too many minutes later, rather more slowly, his body lower to the ground. She also handed him a note about Poppy's lift, which he didn't have the breath to respond to, but put in his pocket with a sort of gasp and a nod.

At ten thirty Poppy was trying out an old coffee-brown piano in need of a polish, a tuner and a damp cloth for its sticky keys. The church hall had become a kind of toddler gym, with tunnels and play mats and a low, chunky slide, pull-along toys and bricks of different textures and sizes. There were hard plastic chairs along the sides for the adults to sit on when they took a break from hand holding, nappy changing, mouth wiping, calming and rescuing. Natalie was in the kitchen end with the kettle. She seemed to know all the names, and in between carrying trays, picked up children who seemed happy to be cuddled, cleaned up or read a story by "Nat-leeee". And she seemed equally happy, even when this attention resulted in soggy drops of biscuit in her perm, or an earring pulled down rather hard like a chain in an old school toilet.

Having established that there were one or two notes that were no more than gummed-up thuds, Poppy ran through a couple of the songs very quietly under the general noise, and was trying to gesture to Natalie that she was ready to begin when Lol burst through the door, followed by a thin woman with short, photo-shoot hair. She removed shades and reached out her arms to grab Lol, who protested because she was en route to the red slide. Kane's mother. Karen. Poppy realised she didn't know anything else about her except that she was "loved up" with someone who was Lol's father but not Kane's. She wore skinny-leg jeans and all her nails were the same ink-blue, including the ones on show in this summer's sandals. But she wasn't nineteen. She must be at least thirty-two.

Natalie put a child down and went to greet her. Poppy had a feeling it might be her first time. She was introduced to some women who were wider, shorter and dressed in looser clothes. Then Natalie must have told people that the singing was going to start because they all scooped up their children and gathered around on a rug in front of the piano, where shakers and tambourines were given out and rattled.

The tunes weren't exactly challenging and the adults sang with enthusiasm, although it was hard to hear many under-four voices except when animal noises were required. Some copied the actions in a bemused, wide-eyed way. Others, the regulars, were whole-hearted and abandoned, especially when these required stamping feet. Poppy enjoyed herself. When the five songs were over, Natalie thanked her and said who she was. Everyone clapped and she saw Kane's mum's shiny mouth make an 'O' of recognition.

"You know my Kane," she said, as Poppy put the music away and closed the lid. Lol was holding onto her bare leg and placing her mouth against it in a wet kiss.

"Yes," said Poppy, and smiled. "He's very good with the donkeys."

"Yeah?" asked his mother. "Good. That's good." She smiled. "Now I get it! I can see why he's been having more showers and nicking Al's scent."

Poppy's mouth formed an "Oh …" that wasn't sure of itself.

"How old are you?"

"Fourteen in October."

She wished she hadn't put it that way. Karen smiled longingly and said she could just about remember.

"Have you got a boyfriend?"

Poppy realised Kane had never asked. She also realised that his mother was likely to report back whatever she said.

"Not yet."

"You won't be short of offers. Like me. But I didn't know then what I know now. Mistakes have to be paid for – well, mine did. But sometimes you get lucky in the end. Lucky or blessed."

She picked up Lol and they rubbed noses, then ears.

"Nice to meet you anyway," she said. "I'm Karen." Lol had noticed a ride-on toy and was leaning out of her arms towards it. "Don't believe everything you hear about Kane. He's doing all right."

But I haven't heard anything about Kane, thought Poppy, as Karen and Lol turned their backs on her for colourful plastic with wheels. Natalie came and thanked her again and said her lift to Highover would be on the way if she wanted to wait outside. It was only once she closed the door on the hall that Poppy appreciated how many smells it shut inside.

Kane smelt nicer because of her! She wished she knew what the saint thing meant, and the father thing – which she suspected was the mistake. Sorrel Golding had made a mistake too, something to do with a man, like Tamarisk with Robert Madison. But Hebe hadn't. Hebe had been in love with Paul, in spite of all the prejudice and difficulty and hate notes.

And her own parents? Were they as happy as that? Her mum was, not just in that smiley American way Poppy's friends noticed, but deeper down. She'd seen it, in her expression when she reached out a hand and stroked the back of her dad's neck as he unwound in front of the TV. David Golding the abandoned baby didn't smile or laugh so much. He kept very busy in his work suits and fell asleep a lot at home. Poppy had never considered whether he was happy, in himself or with her mum, and now that she did it felt like a shock. "Is he depressed or something?" Ed had muttered once, cross because their dad had been cross with him. And now she knew he might be feeling all kinds of things she didn't want to imagine.

Vic was taking his time. Then as the car pulled up in the drive outside the church hall she couldn't think of his real name and wasn't sure she'd ever heard it. She was too far from the board in the churchyard to make it out, so it was just as well that he did the vicarly thing and shook her hand.

"I'm Jonathan," he said, over the music that roared through the open door. "But I won't be offended if you call me Vic. Lanky's done it for thirty odd years."

Vic/Jonathan looked much more solid in his church black, with washed hair fluffy around his dog collar and a colour that had stopped throbbing in his cheeks and spread evenly around his clean, shiny face. He drove faster than Natalie and turned the volume up on Mahler until the car almost vibrated. His eyes were moist as the final movement ended a couple of miles later.

"I'm so sorry, Poppy," he said. "Forgive me. I'd been listening in my study since the third movement started and had to run from the front door to the car so as not to miss anything. Obsessive, I'm afraid. My mother did teach me manners once." He turned the radio off.

"I think it would have been much ruder to talk through it," said Poppy, who'd loved every surge and ache of it. He gave the wheel a slap of pleasure.

"Of course! You felt it too. I married a rock chick, you know! But then you're a flower girl, aren't you? So tell me, are you having a good stay? Natalie tells me you're trying to put together their story. Fascinating stuff, isn't it? Exceptional women."

Poppy felt like an on the spot reporter thrusting a mic at him but she couldn't help it.

"What do you know, Vic? Jonathan?"

Rather less than her, it seemed, about Tamarisk and Hebe. And there he stopped, where Sorrel began, because of course Sorrel was another story, one that was apparently banned or eighteen certificate or classified. Poppy was quite cross until she remembered that vicars had to treat people's personal lives as confidential. He must have sensed that she'd hoped for more and explained that he wasn't born and bred in the area like Lanky and Natalie so he couldn't divulge anything firsthand.

"When I met Nat we were both social workers in Newham. Then once I'd been ordained we got moved around all over the place before this job became available. A final resting place. You can imagine how happy Natalie was to come home."

"Oh," said Poppy, realising she'd assumed all kinds of wrong things and wondering how many more she had in place in her head.

"So I didn't know Sorrel, although I wish I had."

Poppy gave him a grateful look. He'd said the name, in the village where she'd lived. It was as if she finally existed.

"I did get to know your dad, though, as a boy. He'd come to live with Lanky even before I met her. We visited, of course. Lanky and Nat have always been thick as thieves."

He smiled and Poppy smiled back.

"What was Dad like?"

"Lovely lad. Serious-minded, sensitive, imaginative. Helped out in the florist's. Played the violin without strangling any cats."

Poppy wished she could see him more clearly. She also wished he hadn't let the violin go. It was a waste.

"Oh," Vic said, "I found a book this morning. You might be interested. It's mainly photographs. Self-published of course, by a local man who died a while ago, but I never really had the time to give it proper attention. A village history."

It was on the back seat. Poppy managed to reach it, and wiped the dust string from its rim. It didn't seem to have an index so she started flicking through. The church was there, from lots of different angles, and the school, too, along with the same photograph Poppy had seen in the dining room, of Tamarisk when she was still Freer, tall and captive at the back of the crowd. There was a horse and cart on a lane and a pub that no longer existed, with men outside it in caps and shirt sleeves. And one of cows being herded past the post office.

"It wasn't all buttercups and roses in the olden days, Poppy. Don't be fooled. People forget the storms and remember the sunshine, that's all."

Poppy told him school used to be harsh and dull and he agreed. Even when he was growing up, he said, a lot of parents crushed their children, suppressed their own feelings and lived in a kind of tight-lipped, well-mannered denial. There was lots of pretending.

"Apart from your flower girls," he smiled.

"Was that what made them exceptional?" she asked.

"That and their music. I reckon they were brave, passionate women, don't you?"

Poppy realised she felt proud. She looked back to the book but it was a disappointment. She couldn't even find Robert Madison anywhere, and mean though he was, as number one fat cat he should get at least a mention. Then she saw it. Madison – the name jumped out at her. There was a photograph of the house, the one where he'd beaten Hebe. She might have recognised it anyway, from what remained of the outside elegance. It was a boring picture, with no people anywhere, not even a face caught at any of the many windows. But the name was in a caption underneath.

The home of local businessman Robert Madison was used briefly as a mental hospital after his death in 1933. His widow, who founded the hospital against local opposition, called it a Recovery Home. The home closed for lack of funds in 1937, was bought by an American during the war and later turned into flats in the Eighties.

Poppy didn't read it aloud, just to herself. There was so much there, unsaid, that she was silent for a while, processing. Tamarisk might have walked away from the house when she left Robert, but if he'd been angry or humiliated it hadn't stopped him leaving it to her in his will. Because of course, he'd never stopped loving her, in his way.

But Poppy wasn't inclined to forgive Robert anything. He wasn't fit to lie in the shadow of a woman who was so amazing that when she could just have lived it up in the swanky old house with her girls, she'd turned it into a hospital for people who were mentally ill ... like he'd been?

Hebe was right. Tamarisk was magnificent, and these people who opposed her should have been ashamed ...

It was frustrating. It made her want more. Looking down at the book was making her feel sick but Vic said she was welcome to keep it a couple of days. Poppy was trying to piece together the widow and the Recovery Home, the opposition and the war, and whether a captive Tamarisk was free yet, when they arrived in Highover. Vic, who had been leaving her with her thoughts, started to commentate as she closed the book and looked out of the car window.

When Lanky said it wasn't Manchester, she hadn't been kidding. It was a straggly, boxy jumble of a place, with a big, ugly church where the concert would be and the usual chain stores. It wasn't stylish in a shiny, glassy way with fountains, or traditional in the sense that Americans liked. It was just a town, not as well looked after as it should be. Vic had said it had muddled along without ever growing into its own character. Lanky had told her where to find the flower shop that used to be hers, which had had several facelifts since. Vic pointed out the town hall set back from the high street as they crawled past along speed bumps.

Without curves, colour, variation or flourishes, it simply blocked out space with yellow brick and uniform glass. The lawn around it was as manicured as a putting green but level and rectangular as the concrete. Only the dahlias, scarlet and burgundy and orange, with spikes and pompoms and dark button cores, broke the rules and the symmetry. Wild and uneven, irregular and chaotic, Poppy thought they didn't need bees to buzz. But the municipal building behind them looked as if it had bored itself to sleep.

Vic dropped her at the bus station where she could get a bus back. He warned her that she might well need to, if his meetings dragged on, and insisted on giving her a fiver in case. If he hadn't surfaced by two, she would get the 154.

"Thanks!"

Poppy smiled as she stepped out of the car. She looked first for the tights. With a purple pair in her bag she searched next for Lanky's florist's shop. It wasn't too hard to find, between the empty Woolworth store where Natalie used to work as a sixth former in her school holidays, and a coffee shop where people sat outside in the emerging sun. Not the best time for cut flowers, of course, and Poppy wasn't sure the roses would ever unfurl from their tightness, but the cannas were fiery at a price. The woman behind the counter came outside and asked if she could help her, which made her feel guilty for only looking.

"My great aunt used to own this shop in the Seventies," she blurted, and then wished she hadn't.

"Is that right? I suppose people had money for flowers then," said the woman, and lit a cigarette.

"I might come back to buy her some Busy Lizzies later on," said Poppy, because the woman seemed so drab and dark beside the flowers.

"Don't leave it too long, love," said the woman as she moved away. "I might have sold out by then!" She laughed sarcastically. "If you see Elton John on your travels, send him along, will you?"

Poppy smiled and strolled on in search of estate agents. She had the details of the Madison flat in her bag and checked the name at the top, but she passed three others, all quiet as she peered behind the boards with the houses on, before she found it. As soon as she reached it she stopped, wondering why she wanted to find it and what she'd do if Kane was there, and saw her. It was the quest. It had seeped into everything else and turned her into an obsessive like Vic claimed to be, only his was a great music obsession and that was fine and normal. This was ... not.

Poppy crossed the road and walked away in the direction of the town hall. Looking at her reflection in passing, she remembered what Kane's mum had said and asked herself how likely it was that he saw her as anything but a kid. Which she was, and wasn't, both at the same time. And posh with it, as Kane would say, not least because her roots went back to a mansion like Madison House. Well, she liked him regardless of everything outside and around him, every question she couldn't answer and every difference anyone could find to place between them. Kane would have to do the same, or not. She was who she was, like Tamarisk and Hebe before her.

She lengthened her stride and turned into the wide drive that led up to the yellow brick building where sixty-nine years earlier Paul Golding had arrived to defend his position as a young man who wouldn't fight for his country in war time.

Poppy didn't know what she expected from Highover Town Hall. She wanted to see it, absorb it, and imagine, of course. Beyond that ... As she walked in, she felt something like a wave rise high and hold as if it wouldn't fall.

A woman on reception asked whether she could help her. Poppy felt herself shiver as the air conditioning chilled her in her skimpy summer clothes. The place had the quiet serious-mindedness of a library but less life. She wondered what was going on in all the different offices behind the doors, and the labels didn't help much.

"I wanted to see where my great grandfather had to face his conscientious objection tribunal," she said. "Do you know where that would have been?"

The woman looked interested, her official face suddenly alive. She pressed some buttons and waited, then told someone she had a young lady who ... Poppy waited. She said Roger would be here soon and would Poppy like to take a seat.

What else happened at town halls anyway? Poppy was realising how much she didn't know when Roger appeared in a suit and tie and small round glasses, the kind her dad always called John Lennon.

"Hi!" he said, briskly. "School project, is it? Will there be dozens of others wanting to know?"

She assured him it was just her. He took her into an empty room, knocking first just in case. Dust specked the air. It didn't look intimidating, or anything like a court. There was no dock, just tables and chairs, some kind of hanging with a coat of arms, and curtains that were so dry and faded Poppy reckoned they could have been there when Paul Golding made his stand.

"I'm told this would have been the room," he said. "Probably. I'm sure there are statistics about how many there were and all that, but I'd need notice to find out that kind of detail."

Poppy said she didn't need statistics and he looked at his watch and seemed relieved.

"You know they had to register first, at the Job Centre, only they called it the Employment Exchange then. It can't have been very comfortable because they had a line for the

COs in amongst the lines of people declaring themselves for military service. Then they waited to be summoned to a tribunal here. They'd see a few in one day. Apparently anyone seen after lunch at the pub had a better chance of exemption."

"Exemption from ..." Poppy couldn't think of the phrase straight away. "Military service?"

He gave her a look a bit like Ed might and she wouldn't have been surprised if he'd said, *No – exemption from washing up, derrrr!* He asked what year she was in and she blushed. She'd only wanted to be sure. It was complicated. When she said Year 9 next term he seemed surprised, as people often did, because of her height.

"Well, as you see there's not a lot to show you. Was there anything in particular?"

"It's a case in 1943," she said. "My great grandfather, Paul Golding."

"Well, as I said, there will be records but I'm not sure ..." He looked at his watch again. "There's somewhere I have to be, strictly speaking. If you want to put your request in writing, I dare say it might be possible."

Poppy gave him one of her non-committal *hmms*. She should have known it would be a waste of time. He held the door open for her. As they returned to the reception area he turned to her with a smile.

"He didn't marry some Frenchwoman? A music hall singer?" Poppy might have objected but thought that was close enough. "There was some notorious case my predecessor told me about. He was a history buff." Roger paused and she could see him trying to dredge up the interesting things that had got buried under data. "This was a big local story at the time. Was she old enough to be his ... a lot older than him?"

"Yes," said Poppy, although he was annoying her now.

"I can't remember any more but it'll be on record. Freedom of information and all that."

With another look at his watch he was gone. Poppy stood a moment in reception, and as she moved towards the double doors she heard him reappear, leaning against the door into the corridor.

"She got him off anyway!" he called.

Poppy opened her mouth in protest.

"No!" she shouted, so that an elderly woman passing by gave her a hard, *young people today!* kind of stare. "He wasn't charged with anything! It wasn't a trial!"

But Roger didn't hear. As Poppy walked away she told herself it wasn't the soldiers and sailors and pilots who had to defend their decision to join up, but the COs who were on the spot, being examined, and judged.

There was a bench by the wall looking onto the road, where nobody in their right mind would choose to sit, but it reminded her of the rose bed she'd seen behind the room where Roger had taken her, through the dusty curtains that looked as if they might shred at a touch, the scarlet petals making the fabric look anaemic. She walked round the side of the building to see them close up. It was a habit. Her dad said roses these days never smelt like they used to.

Poppy wasn't entirely sure she should be there, but it wasn't chained off and nobody walking about their own business seemed to care. She smelt the roses but they proved her father's point. The clouds were quite menacing all of a sudden. She was going to put the town hall behind her, and try to forget how annoying Roger had been, but the rain changed her mind. Not that it was rain at first, just thunder, a boulder cracking away from some cliff in the sky. And almost straight away, a quick stab of lightning seemed to strike on both sides of her, inside and out, not just across the lawn but through the glass. Just a reflection, of course, but it drew her gaze through the window. She was looking at the room where Paul Golding had stood, and as the rain began to fall sharply on her head and bare arms, she saw him, his back to her, his hair short, wearing the same oversized suit he'd recycled for the wedding. Centre stage. And something in Poppy recognised that there was no point in resisting or even analysing, because it was happening again and some part of her had hung around, taking shelter in the ordinariness of the rain and the flowers and the yellow brick, in the hope that it might.

She didn't see the faces of the tribunal members, at least not clearly. Paul was in a strip, cut away from the rest, so that in the centre of the dull modern room an excerpt from another time lay like a cutting on a floor. But through the rain she heard their voices, crackling like an old recording.

Can you look your friends in the eye, without feeling you are letting them down?

You're very young to have thought this through. Has someone prejudiced you?

If you don't believe in killing, why is it that you're not a vegetarian?

Christians have fought just wars for two thousand years. Is your moral high ground more elevated, or is it simply squeamishness?

Have you ever considered that your opposition might be fear, dressed up as something superior?

But as the questions flowed like rain through a gutter, the words passed from the mouths of well-spoken men into a softer voice close by, as if Hebe stood there beside her in the rain. She thought she felt the brush of a skirt against her legs, not damp but warm and dry. There was a voice without a body, and it felt so close it might have been under her skin, just where the veins throbbed.

We'd practised. Mother had helped, but even she hadn't anticipated. He spoke of his faith. They questioned his education. They quoted archbishops, and asked him to name the twelve apostles. I watched him drowning in his quietness and his youth. They twisted and turned and jumped him from behind.

Is it because you are entangled, they asked, in a love affair? What about love of your country? Isn't that the deepest, most enduring love? An accident of birth, he said, a responsibility, not a choice. He loved beauty, he told them, goodness and truth, and Jesus who represents the kind of love that will die for others but never kill.

The rain had thickened. Poppy's beaded hair began to drip cold, the thin fabric on her shoulders soaked and clinging. Lightning flashed, and this time it seemed to divide the scene in the room with its dark suits and grey smoke. There, through dribbling rain on glass, she saw Hebe take shape like a cloud curved by wind. She was tall and trim, her hair scooped and netted under a feathered hat that undulated down over one eye, her shoes a darker green than her jacketed dress. She rose, her hands gloved and holding the table a moment before she clasped them together. Like the faceless panel with their upholstered shoulders and shorn red necks breaking away into air, she felt herself enclosed in Hebe's gaze.

My name is Hebe Madison. I am the woman with whom, as you have said, Paul Golding is entangled in a love affair. I will soon become his wife. My father was a rich and successful man, highly respected in this town; I was not proud of his money or his position. I am acclaimed as an accomplished musician; I am not proud of my talent. But I am proud of Paul.

What has he done to earn my admiration? Studied hard? He has. Taken care of his little sister, with whom he was evacuated? He has, though he had to do battle with the bureaucracy that separated them, and win. Earned the respect of the community and behaved with a dignity beyond his years? He has. There can be no illustrious CV. He is eighteen years old. But already he does something that most respectable people twice his age have not yet begun to do. It is honourable, but so courageous and rare that most of us shuffle through life unable or unwilling to try.

Paul Golding holds true to himself and the light inside him. He keeps it burning in the rain that falls so hard on all of us, against an angry wind, and the currents of doubt that blow in low underneath the door when his father calls or his friends ask questions. It may flicker once in a while. But it is not extinguished. It is younger and newer than ours, but he will not give it up. He will not pretend it is other than it is. He will not keep it hidden. He must own it, because it is his soul. Not yours, or the King's or the Prime Minister's soul, not mine or his father's, but his own, the only one he has, the only one he can offer to God and His world. It is this soul that makes him who he is, a young man who has no choice but to stand before you now ...

The words were washed away by rain, beaten under by the rhythm. There was no silence for them to fill, no close ups on faces, no movie scene music. Just the rain, and the room inside streaking grey like the sky, while Poppy felt herself shiver, and wrapped herself like an old stone figure on a tomb.

Sorrel? Sorrel!

It sounded almost like a mother calling a child, or the owner of a lost dog. Or a gust of wind ripping across a brand new puddle. Stirring, Poppy felt as if she had stumbled into reality after sleep. There was no nightmare to shake off. She remembered what Kath Golding had said. It was *fine*. A triumph. But whatever she called it, it flooded her and she felt heavy with it, as if it rushed around her still, hot and roaring, and she didn't know whether she wanted it to cool and trickle away.

There was a patch of blue sky over the offices across the damp, black road with its unbroken traffic crawling on into town. The rain was nearly over and the sun would dry her clothes. She moved quickly, leaving the yellow building behind her, and waited for a chance to cross with no idea where to go.

Kane stepped out of a bakery with a bread roll in a paper bag, and one end of its crust in his mouth. She stopped, and waited while he chewed, a smile lifting at the edges of his working mouth.

"You're drenched," he said. "Most people sheltered. It's a town. It's got roofs."

"I was smelling roses," she said, her voice tearful, "but they had no scent."

For a moment she thought he might laugh. But he didn't. His eyes looked for an explanation she couldn't give and he didn't ask. Poppy felt grateful, but it was hard to smile, partly because she was shivering.

"Come with me," he said.

The hairdresser's was quiet. It was where his mum worked, part-time, and although it was her day off, he said, Della wouldn't mind.

Poppy sat in a swivel chair being warmed by hot current, body as well as hair, which Della blow-dried with a little leave-in conditioner and a few compliments about colour and texture and body. Kane sat with his legs stretched out at the back, flicking through magazines he wasn't reading. More than once she caught him looking up and into the mirror she faced. Ten minutes later they stepped out into sunshine and Poppy's phone bleeped. Vic was finished. Second meeting cancelled. He was at the bus station. Was she ready?

To her surprise, Kane accepted a lift as far as Eddington, said "All right?" as he climbed in the back behind Poppy and didn't seem fazed by the dog collar or the violins.

"How are things, Kane?" asked Vic, calling back.

"All right, thanks," he said. "Getting there."

Poppy guessed Vic understood what that meant and doubted whether either of them would tell her if she asked.

"Going back to school in September? Any decisions yet?"

"Maybe. If they'll have me. I'll try to sit the exams this time."

Had he walked out, or just not turned up? Perhaps he'd been ill as well as in trouble. They all knew, except her.

"Excellent. Very good news."

"I want to work with animals and you need qualifications."

"Ah, yes. So the donkeys …?"

"They were your idea, right?"

"Might have been!" grinned Vic.

"Sound," said Kane.

Poppy didn't mind being invisible. In fact, she was hoping they'd forget her altogether and let slip all the stuff she wasn't supposed to know. But Vic was too vicarly for that.

"Poppy," he said, with a smile, "what about you?"

"I want to be a musician."

"Hip hop?" came from the back.

Vic grinned into the mirror.

"You must play the piano tonight," he told Poppy. "Pre-dinner treat. And after-dinner treat! But how was Highover? Any luck at the town hall?"

"Yes," she answered rather slowly, considering. "My great grandmother Hebe spoke up as a witness for Paul Golding at the tribunal. He was given ..." Poppy couldn't remember the word and she'd look stupid without it. "Exemption," she finished, just as Vic started to supply it. "It was a passionate speech," she added. "She was irresistible."

Was it true? Or had the panel just had lunch at the pub? Some things could never be proved, or even glimpsed. But Hebe was amazing, stupendous and extraordinary. She loved her. She loved her love. The tide inside Poppy felt blue and sunlit now and she felt ready to let it carry her away.

The other two allowed her to sit and smile to herself. Maybe Vic thought she was barking. But Kane couldn't have thought the same, because when they stopped in Eddington, and Poppy got up to let him out, he said thank you for the lift, and before she could sit down and strap herself in again, he asked her if she'd like to stop by and see Lol.

Poppy looked in at Vic.

"Yes. Great," she said, trying not to sound too desperate.

"Shall we say half an hour?" Vic suggested. "I'll tell Lanky you'll get the two o'clock bus, shall I?"

"I'll walk back with her," offered Kane. "I want to check on Midge and Ben anyway."

Vic didn't seem alarmed. He smiled, and drove off with the volume swelling.

"What happened?" asked Kane.

She didn't answer because she didn't know where to begin, or why for the first time the ghosts had hung on after it was all over, replaying in her head. Was it because this felt like the end, the last encounter, the one that lingered and gathered around it all the rest? The one that made the total too much, tipping the weight over the limit? She knew her eyes were full, because they spilt a little, and when she'd wiped them, he took the damp hand in his.

"We need another hairdryer," he said.

Chapter Ten

As they walked towards Kane's estate he chatted. Poppy knew he was giving her time to decide, to tell or not tell. She hadn't decided. She just told herself not to cry, not over the past, over milk that wasn't just spilt but congealed and rank and practically a museum piece.

"Vicathan's all right," he said. "Gave us the benefit of the doubt, didn't he? He thinks the best of people. But then that's his job, I suppose."

She remembered the book in her bag and produced it, finding the page with the photo. But it was hard to look and walk at the same time so they sat on a verge at the edge of the estate. She spread her skirt underneath her legs, hoping the raindrops left behind on the grass wouldn't give her a damp patch.

Kane said Tamarisk was ahead of her time because most people were scared of mental illness then. Poppy told him about Roger and the room, and let him think the colours and sounds had come along with the jumbled up facts. He had a good look at all the photographs, recognising a few places and muttering that history was quite interesting if you got inside it. He didn't suggest that she was way too deep down and needed to drag herself up and out. Maybe, she thought, he was leaving her the space to work that out for herself. In her mind she tried out an opening: *Kane, the past keeps pulling me in and I don't know whether I can stop, or resist, or let go. Or what I'd do if it was over.*

While he flicked through, Poppy saw a bus draw up further back along the street, and noticed a man getting off. He carried a backpack which he was quick to remove, stretching and wincing as if it was full of bricks. But Poppy didn't mention it and Kane didn't look up at the sound of footsteps. Not until the smoke from the man's cigarette drifted towards them ahead of him, and his shadow leant across.

"Hullo, son."

Kane didn't speak at first. He closed the book and Poppy took it, slipping it into her bag. He stood up. The man was no taller than him, thicker round the waist and broader-shouldered, with slightly more than a stubble of darker hair. He had a tattoo on one arm, which must have been hours' worth of lines and shapes, and a message too, but Poppy couldn't read it. She thought at first that she wouldn't have known, that there was nothing to connect them. Yet there was something in the way he stood, and then in his half-smile as he held out an arm. Kane's hands were in his pockets. The arm touched his back very briefly, as if it was going to be a friendly slap but got recalled. At once Kane's shoulders hunched, narrowing him, caving him in. Then he straightened.

"You're meant to call first," he said. "Mum …"

"Is he there?"

"I don't know. You can't just turn up."

"Who's your girlfriend?" his father asked, glancing at Poppy, the whole length of her.

"Too good for you."

It was an accusation. She hadn't heard that voice since the phone call. His father stubbed out his cigarette and smiled at Poppy.

"Too good for you too," he told his son.

"Yeah," said Kane. It was muttered, like an admission he couldn't help, or had to make.

"Gary Bradley, love," said his father, and winked.

"I'm Poppy," she said, sounding neutral, but edging closer to Kane as if to make it clear: she was with him and on his side. Kane was scraping stones with his foot. He looked up at her, wide-eyed, and she realised he didn't know what to do.

"Pretty name for a pretty girl," said Gary Bradley. It came out like a line in a script that he'd practised but couldn't get to sound natural in spite of the grin.

"Jonathan – the vicar – is coming to pick me up from Kane's place some time soon," said Poppy, looking at her watch. "He's my godfather."

"Is that right? Connections in high places, eh?"

"Mum's got God," said Kane. "She's made him a cake."

Gary Bradley spluttered and swore, then apologised to Poppy.

"Let's hope God's like a goat, then," he muttered. "Eats anything, I mean. Even your mother's baking."

"Things have changed," said Kane.

"I can see that." Gary Bradley picked up his backpack and slung it on, adjusting his shoulders and straightening up to take the weight. "It's prisoners who are supposed to get God."

A bus drew up on the other side of the road. He raised his hand towards the driver and hurried across, looking back and giving them a one-move turn of the hand like unscrewing a light bulb.

"Tell your mum we need to meet up – in between choir practice and bible study." He called again from the opposite kerb. "Suppose I've changed too?"

They saw him climb on board. Kane pulled Poppy away, as if he'd seen enough. She heard the bus pull off but neither of them watched it go.

"God," muttered Kane. "Mum's gonna freak."

"Can I do anything? What can I do?"

"You were a total star. Genius. I didn't know how to head him off," he told her, talking and walking quickly. "Except with an iron bar to the head." He looked down into her face, checking. "Joke. Kind of."

"I know."

He stopped suddenly.

"Look, can you get back on your own? I'm sorry. But I need … Well, you see how things are. Tell Jonathan, will you? He knows what happened. He might be able … I don't know. I'll text, yeah?"

He squeezed her hand very lightly and let it go. Poppy nodded.

"Tell your mum not to worry," she told him hopefully.

He looked as if he thought that would be a waste of breath, but he pulled together a quick smile.

"Don't you worry, either! Don't be distracted from the quest!"

He turned then, and ran, much faster than his father had managed. Poppy felt the fear that drew him home.

Poppy told Vic what had happened, and he said he'd do what he could. He was calm and tried to reassure her, telling her she'd been very quick-witted and resourceful. Poppy knew he was being kind; she just wished she wasn't the only one being treated like a child. She wouldn't have been surprised to discover that Lol understood all this rather better than she did.

She helped with the donkeys. They'd had to come in from the rain, but smelt different, the dampness clinging. Midge was responding well to the Bach flowers and had moved freely, a few more centimetres out into the wild world. Poppy sat with Lanky talking memorials, but she seemed to have used up all her ideas for the day. Her only text message was a disappointment: Min had fallen out with Katie again and she wished they wouldn't, but she couldn't be bothered to react, not today. Then her mum called, just before they went round to dinner at the vicarage, and it was one of those conversations they had, now and then, when she batted back one word answers and just couldn't manage more. Which forced Anna Beth to ask lots of questions for the sake of talking, finishing with the same one twice: "Honey, are you okay?"

She knew her mother knew – not what, of course, but something. Then Lanky had a quick word and reassured her somehow. Poppy almost opted out of dinner with a headache, but she wanted to play the piano. According to Lanky it was neglected but a good one, and now that she'd had a break from all the practice she was missing the music and how it made her feel – not so young or stupid after all.

Before they walked over under an umbrella, she texted Kane. No answer. She wanted to do for him what Hebe had done for Paul Golding. *I believe in you, Kane,* Poppy told him, not in words, not in text speak, but in her head, picturing him running, long and gangly, towards the estate. She squeezed the hand he had held, trying to bring back the feeling.

Natalie and Vic were cuddling in the kitchen when they walked in through the back door.

"Shall we go away, cough and come back in?" asked Lanky, shaking her head.

"Are we an embarrassment, Poppy?" smiled Natalie, kissing Vic's cheek and pulling away.

"No," she said. "It's nice."

"Enough to put anyone off their food," muttered Lanky. "Red wine would be lovely, thank you, Natalie. Kind of you to ask."

Natalie, who didn't seem to mind any amount of rudeness from her best friend, simply asked sweetly whether she wanted it over her head or down the back of her neck. She was bouncy and attentive towards all three of them, but especially Poppy. She invited her to play almost at once, probably because she'd seen her eyeing the piano. And it was a good one, even though Natalie said she hadn't played a pitiful boogie-woogie blues for months and if she didn't pull herself together she'd be left with a repertoire of Chopsticks.

Poppy played a Chopin prelude – a little rustily at first but it came together gradually and she nearly lost track of everything else in the rush of exhilaration that overwhelmed it all. There was something that clung on, that didn't get banished by the music but inhabited it. In spite of the early mistakes it was the best she'd ever played.

Looking up, she breathed deeply. Lanky stamped her feet and looked as if she could do with a football supporter's rattle.

"I didn't realise," said Vic, "not fully ..."

She had moved him and she wondered whether she could move Kane too, one day. But she hoped that if he needed to blow his nose like Vic did, it would be rather more musical. Lanky told him to stop scaring the donkeys and get on with saying grace so they could eat. He cleared his throat to thank God for good food and good company, and the joy of music.

The conversation that followed wasn't the sort that excluded Poppy. Natalie filled it with anecdotes about the days when she and Lanky had been best friends at school. Lanky accused Natalie of being teacher's favourite every year, of wearing more eyeliner than Cleopatra, mini skirts up to her armpits and trying to look like Diana Dors without the boobs. When Poppy looked blank Vic explained she was a movie siren.

Lanky, apparently, was always attempting daredevil stunts.

"One time," said Natalie, "Lank was dared to throw herself out of a first floor window. She couldn't resist, could she? After all, she was school champion at both the jumps, long and high."

"This was both," remembered Lanky, "but I needed a whole new technique."

"She landed in the roses right outside the Head's office! Another entry in the black book for Amelanchier Golding!"

"Ouch!" said Lanky, whose bottom seemed to be reliving the episode as she fidgeted on the dining chair.

"My heart bled for the roses," said Natalie. "Lank's bottom just bled."

Vic laughed so loudly that Poppy wondered whether it was a party piece, an old story that got funnier with familiarity.

"It was quite a different world then. But we did want to change it."

"Did you worry about the world?" asked Poppy, because she did, more than she used to, close-up and far away.

"Oh yes," said Natalie. "We were CND, weren't we?"

All three of them had been on demonstrations, calling on the government to ban the bomb. Lanky said that long before that, her whole family had marched from London to Aldermaston in '58, when she was six. Everyone was singing *When The Saints Go Marching In*. It had felt like a very long walk and she'd held on tightly to her big sister's hand all the way. The memory just slipped out. No S-word. Just Sorrel left silently hanging in the space above the table like a spirit at a séance.

While Lanky stacked up plates, Vic asked Poppy to tell Natalie about the town hall and the tribunal. Crisis averted, thought Poppy. She started with the ordinary bits she'd got from Roger.

"He dug land drains," said Lanky. "They came calling for him at five every morning. He wanted to be a teacher but they wouldn't let him, not then." She smiled at Poppy. "But he never told me what happened at the tribunal. Neither of them did."

So Poppy told them about Hebe's speech and Paul Golding's soul, trying to remember certain words just as she'd heard them. She felt her own heat seeping out through her skin as she spoke, her head mostly downward to the tablecloth where she stroked criss-cross patterns with her fork. They all listened very intently even though they must have thought she was embellishing a very bare kind of truth. Lanky moved her shiny napkin ring around, studying its golden elephants. Then when Poppy had finished, she touched her arm very gently and murmured that she was sure that was it, exactly.

"That seems just right to me, Poppy," she added, having wiped her mouth slowly with a best napkin. "I couldn't have scripted it better."

After dessert Poppy played again by request. The piece was a film score to a movie her dad wouldn't let her see, but fun to play and part of her campaign to make him change his mind. Then she went to the toilet and texted Kane.

RUOK?

She didn't add any kisses or smileys but willed him to reply. Nothing came, although she discreetly checked the pocket in her bag several times during the rest of the evening.

"See you tomorrow for Mary's bash," said Lanky as they left. "No doctrine, please, just some of my father's soul."

Poppy had a feeling Kane wouldn't be there. She kept her phone on all night, but she couldn't sleep. In the end, some time before midnight, she crept downstairs and turned on the television, very low volume with the door shut. Lanky didn't have many channels, and there didn't seem to be anything that wasn't for people with an I.Q. of seven – or a hundred and eighty. After a lot of hopping, she settled for a documentary in a series about the Sixties, because that was when Lanky and Natalie were schoolgirls, and she wondered whether she might get a glimpse of Diana Dors, siren. It was about powerful figures in the background who never became household names. She'd seen the fashions and hairstyles before, but it was hard to picture Lanky looking like the women they showed slinking down Carnaby Street or the King's Road.

Apparently Swinging London wasn't just about mini skirts and bell-bottoms and go-go dancers. Behind that exterior it was a gangster's paradise. There was a club owner who knew all the celebs and groovers at the time, and was handsome and charming but ran protection rackets. He made millions out of the drugs trade and providing expensive call girls. Marty something, an ordinary name and nothing special to look at as far as Poppy could see, with his hair and everything else too slick. There was black and white film of actresses dancing at his clubs, looking as if they were afraid their hair would collapse if they moved more than one body part at a time. And as if they wanted people to admire their hands.

She was more than convinced that this Marty White guy was a total creep when a tabloid headline came on screen. He died one night in suspicious circumstances, and no one ever faced trial, but the police were pretty sure that it was murder and there was no shortage of suspects. Poppy thought it was interesting to see a seamy side of the peace and love era, and to think that her dad was born the year the guy was killed, but she'd had enough. She hoped she might sleep, even though Kane still hadn't texted. She reached for the remote, but as she clicked it off the last image showed a still of Marty on the night he died, posing behind the scenes at one of his clubs with a crowd of glamorous girls, two of them on his knees with long legs crossed and ending in white boots.

Poppy clicked it back but the shot had gone. The commentary about models and dancers had died away on the words *blow to the head* and all that was left was the question that the voiceover actor said might never be answered. The tallest girl, with a CND symbol round her neck, had disappeared with the rest into a blank screen.

She didn't know. She couldn't be sure. But she felt it anyway. Sorrel Golding, smiling to camera, just as she had with her little sister Lanky in the pictures under the bed. A little older, but not much. A little more make-up, but the same light in her face. And yes, she looked like her. Like Poppy herself might have looked, at that age, at that time.

"Don't be so stupid!" she cried out loud, her voice breaking. She leaned over to turn off at the plug, continuing to talk to herself internally.

Enough drama already. And perhaps, for Kane, enough law-breaking one way or another. Sorrel wouldn't hang around with anyone so creepy or do anything Hebe and Paul couldn't be proud of. Girls all looked like that in the Sixties. Her brothers would call her deranged and she wouldn't have much of a defence.

Sleep, she told herself, back in bed. Again and again she tried common sense likelihood and probability theory. She accused herself of wishing and hoping, and seizing on random flickers of some kind of chance. And then of denying truth when it was sharp as flint in her hand. Impatient and exhausted, she ridiculed herself and tried to forget. Donkey names didn't work and she fell asleep listing made-up names of made-up Sixties glamour girls: Kim Michelle, Gina Lamour, Marilyn Carlotti, Mia Darling, Lola Genesis ...

Chapter Eleven

When Poppy woke again it was just after five and there were no messages on her phone. Her head began to feel crowded as she stared at the clock and mobile and the thin light through the gap in the curtains.

From the bathroom she crept into Lanky's office. It was the smallest bedroom. There were books tilting, angling, piled and scattered all over every surface including the floor, along with papers and torn-off scraps of envelopes with numbers or lists scribbled on the back of them. Pen and pencil tips poked out from underneath this debris like nervous mice. The window at the end was partially blocked by bent and dusty cardboard wallets, and inside one of the rimmed mugs waiting to be washed up, a folded banana skin was trying to decompose. Obviously Natalie hadn't been allowed in this room with her rubber gloves and eco spray.

Poppy couldn't help herself. Quietly she removed and dealt with the more visible health hazards. Then, with a mug of tea in hand, she sat down at the computer. It wasn't what Tim would call cool and Ed might have another word for it. But Lanky spent a lot of time on it, so in spite of its age, clunkiness and grubby surfaces it must function up to a point.

It took so long to get started it reminded her of Ed. She was beginning to miss him and wondering how that had happened. Poppy knew her brain had gone into a kind of busy escape mode. She felt as if she'd dreamed about the things she didn't want to think. For now she just wanted a task and this was the obvious one.

She was about to enter one name when she thought she might as well try another, just in case. Sorrel Golding. Nothing. Okay. She told herself that must be good. Marty White, she tapped in. Go.

First one up, though Britain must have had a few over the years. She knew this was the one because the text underneath had the words gangland and Sixties. And murder too. She clicked and up came a newspaper article from the day after his body was found in an East End side street.

... Employees said he left The Hippolyta Club around one a.m. in his own car... discovered by the kerb ... police alerted by anonymous female caller ... alcohol level ... heart attack ... police treating death as suspicious ... blow to the head.

There was a photograph – the same photograph, the last one of Marty alive. No names.

Another article from a few days later talked about suspects, grudges, criminal investigations into Marty White's businesses and the unsolved murder of a bar manager in which police thought he was implicated. Among those interviewed were bouncers, waiting staff, dancers, singers and hostesses at the Hippolyta and his other clubs. But the police had been unable to trace all of them and were asking whether anyone knew the whereabouts of Deirdre Scott, Ham Tyler ... or Sorrel Ann Silver.

Poppy was sweating under a hot nightie. She looked up from the screen to the window onto the path up to the sanctuary, and the hill rising in a soft-edged dome. Not a lot of room for doubt, then. Not that she'd ever felt any, not for long, however hard she'd wanted to.

Poppy tried to find her place, reading down. It seemed to be the last entry, winding things up. ...*overlooked evidence ... missing wristwatch ... victim of robbery ... many enemies ... doubts remain ... case closed* ...

Lanky stood behind her, cutting across like a second image in a double-exposure photograph, tying the towelling belt round her dressing gown.

"Poppy," she said, her voice deep and scratchy. "What exactly do you think you're doing?"

Poppy spun round on the swivel chair, but not before she'd clicked off.

"Just researching ..."

It sounded so lame and childish and nervous with it. Poppy wanted to turn her head away again and cover her ears but she knew she had to try to look Lanky in the eye.

"This was all a mistake, Poppy, you coming here like Hercule Poirot, poking around into things that are best left alone ..."

Lanky looked exhausted. She sounded exhausted. Poppy felt guilty and defiant at the same time. And she had to know, but she knew she had no right to ask. It was some kind of bad joke, all of it. Have you heard the one about the missing grandma on the run from the law ...?

"I suppose you've found out about Marty White?" Lanky asked, but she wasn't Lanky now, she was Amelanchier Jones and she was as hard as a donkey's kick.

"I ..."

"Don't let this make a liar of you, Poppy!"

Poppy was close to crying. She wasn't sure she could protest without giving in to it. She started to shut down the computer, just to turn away from Lanky's face, to think, to give herself time. Behind her she heard her great aunt walk away, heard her in the bathroom, heard her slowness and the heaviness of her breathing and how deep it went. She heard her go downstairs, still dragging the bad leg just a fraction behind, and click the kettle on. Outside Jerry did his cockerel thing, braying loudly in case anyone in the village was still asleep.

Poppy looked down on the flower beds and beyond to the daisies scattering the hillside like tiny polka dots. She leaned down to the plug and turned the computer off, then made her way downstairs, not too lightly but not fearfully either. Lanky sat facing the kitchen doorway as she walked through. A thin plume of steam rose from her mug and broke up around her face. It wasn't a morning face any more. The muscles were wide awake.

"I haven't done anything wrong," said Poppy, glad to find her voice stronger than it might have been. "There was a programme on last night, when I couldn't sleep. I found it by accident, channel-hopping. It's not a lie."

"Sit down and tell me," said Lanky quietly, pulling out a red chair.

Poppy told her what she'd seen and heard, which wasn't much, and what she'd found online. She said the name, the fake one, the stage one, whatever it was. Sorrel Ann Silver.

"Then you know almost as much as I do." She drank some coffee, and tried to smile, but not very successfully. "What can I tell you, Poppy? That Sorrel didn't kill anyone, couldn't, not to save her life. Daddy's girl, always was, soft about animals, babies ..." Lanky stopped and breathed out. The word carried weight and she let it settle.

"The police did want to see her, because of the photo, because she was at the club that night, and because she disappeared. I don't know why. They came to the house. My poor parents! But we all knew, and they told them, that Sorrel was innocent, at least of any crime. She's your grandmother, Poppy. You need to have some faith."

"I do!" cried Poppy. "She's alive, isn't she, somewhere?"

Lanky took a very deep breath.

"I think so, yes. I don't know for sure. But I like to think ... well, I'd feel it, if she died. I adored her, you see."

It wasn't a Lanky sort of word. Adored. Poppy felt its strength as the volume lowered to accommodate it.

"I didn't want to upset you, Lanky. Or Dad."

"Some of the rest of it is his story too. It has to be his choice to tell it with me, and he will, one day, maybe soon."

Lanky looked vaguely around the room. Poppy sensed she'd given enough, wanted a distraction, a way out, an end.

"Why did she go to London in the first place, instead of going to university, or music college?"

Lanky shook her head as if she'd asked the question again and again and never known the answer.

"All I can tell you is that when she left for London, she had to sneak away from an empty house and leave a note. My parents didn't know how to tell me. I was your age, younger. They knew I worshipped her."

181

"Was it fame and fortune?" asked Poppy. "Big city, bright lights, all that?"

"Village girl seeks other life. Some fool told her she could be a model. She was beautiful without all the make-up, of course, but with it, she had the look. She wrote to me as well as Mum and Dad, and I don't know what she told them in those letters, because they didn't talk about it much and they didn't keep them. Which tells you a lot."

Poppy nodded as if she understood. They loved her. Sometimes it was hard with parents to give enough love back.

"She had a job singing in a club, which she said was more fun than the photo shoots, and she mentioned a chance of a recording contract." Lanky stirred her tea round and round, watching the spoon. "She took her violin with her, and her guitar too. I didn't know anything about Marty White, not until long after he died. I think Dad guessed he was no good. It was the cancer that killed my father but from the day Sorrel left I don't think he was ever happy again. I wasn't the only one who adored her."

"Paul and Hebe died the year Dad was eleven," said Poppy. Even the Year Two family tree had told her that much.

"And I was twenty-one. I hardly felt grown up, even though Derek and I were newly-wed. I think you've worked out that my mother was brave. She was very strong, but not physically. After my father died, she was suddenly frail. And mourning as much as anyone's ever mourned. But she didn't want to die, not with Sorrel still needing her, wherever she was, and your dad still young. She wanted to fight. She just didn't have anything left."

Poppy could see it was hard for Lanky to remember. She couldn't imagine losing her own parents, and both in the same year. And she understood now, or at least she understood a little of everything they didn't want her to know or feel.

"I'm sorry, Lanky," she said, and she reached out a hand to touch hers, big and still on the wooden table.

"It's all right, Poppy. You were spot on. You haven't done anything wrong."

Lanky sprang up then, and made toast. Poppy knew where to find Natalie's home-made jam, the local honey and sugar-free marmalade. They talked about eggs, fresh from the neighbours, and raised the whole range of options, but neither of them wanted any. They ate in silence for a while.

"It looked as if Marty White had fallen down some steps, near where they found him. They never did discover, as far as I know, who he was visiting there, and it wasn't anywhere near Sorrel's flat. She'd hinted she had a boyfriend but I don't believe she'd let a man like Marty White go near her. I followed developments for a while, in the papers, but it soon went quiet. The police gave up in the end."

Poppy just nodded. She wished she'd never heard of Marty White. She didn't ask the obvious: why Sorrel hadn't come back after that, written at least, wanted to see her son. She guessed that was hardest of all for her father and Lanky to understand. She pictured the Sorrel Ann Silver photo but the smile told nothing.

"Well," said Lanky, wiping butter from her top lip with the side of her forefinger, "we've got Mary to send off. Hungry donkeys out there. Natalie will be round to disinfect us as we sit."

Poppy wanted to help as much as she could. She'd be home soon. And she wasn't sure whether they could count on Kane. She fetched the mobile from Lanky's office where she'd left it but there were no messages.

"Kane will be all right, Poppy. Don't worry about all that. His mum's in good shape now, you know. Al's a good bloke, loves her to bits. The pair of them have started taking Lol to church …"

"She really has got God?"

"Must have. I don't suppose she fancies old Vic! Whatever floats your boat, eh?"

Poppy couldn't quite imagine Karen singing hymns but it was interesting. Another false assumption.

"But Kane's dad?"

"Ah," said Lanky at the back door as they both put their boots on. "Not such a good bloke. But Vic would say there's such a thing as repentance. Second chances, you know?"

Poppy remembered he'd said he might have changed. But he'd said other things, shown other faces. She thought some assumptions were instinct and they were dead right, even when it would be better if they weren't.

"That's what Kane had and he's been a diamond. Took things hard for a while but he's doing fine. Don't lose sleep over him."

I can't help it, thought Poppy, but she knew that wasn't what Lanky wanted to hear.

"He'll tell you all about it, I dare say. But don't count on it, or him, or anything but yourself and the people who really love you."

Lanky closed the door and they walked up to feed the donkeys.

Mary's send-off, as Lanky put it, was a celebratory event consisting of the sprinkling of her ashes on the rose bed, followed by the placing of a slice of wood carved with her name among the other memorials. Vic said a very short prayer about her resting in peace and Lanky added that if she had another life ahead, then let it be a good one with lifelong love. Then Vic played a CD of one of Beethoven's last sonatas, at which point Natalie cried.

"Take no notice," Lanky told Poppy. "She does this every time. She'd cry if we played *The Teddy Bears' Picnic*."

It was Poppy's job, as the flower girl, to lay some dahlias by the memorial. And that was that.

"All funerals should be like this one," Lanky told Vic as they lifted the heads they had lowered in respect.

"She says that every time," Natalie told Poppy, and Vic excused himself, saying he had things to do.

Poppy hoped that whatever he was doing would help Kane and Karen, Lol and Al. But even though she'd recharged her phone there was nothing waiting for her when she retrieved it after the ceremony.

Around lunchtime Anna Beth called her and said they'd seen more pictures of Nick on Facebook and she was sure he was in love. She wished Poppy could see them. When Poppy mentioned it to Lanky, assuming that Facebook would be considered a lot of mindless frothy media nonsense and that the technology in the office wouldn't be up to it, she had a surprise. Otherwise known as another false assumption.

"I'm on Facebook, for my sins. Derek's idea when he was ill and needed something to occupy him. Never used to touch it but it's been useful a few times with the donkeys. Networking, they call it, don't they?"

They managed to find the photos of Nick and the girlfriend, which was strange but fun. Poppy hadn't persuaded her parents yet that she should be on it, but maybe now they'd appreciate how useful it could be.

"Lanky," she said suddenly, just as they were going to exit and make more tea, "can I try to find Kane?"

"Oh, he asked me to be a friend ages ago," said Lanky, and let Poppy leave him a message, discreetly leaving the room so she could do it privately but telling her, "No kisses on the end."

Worried about U. Call Poppy.

Well, she couldn't help it if it sounded motherly or big sisterly. She was worried. It was the truth.

"Lanky ..." she started to call, but the music was loud downstairs and besides, she thought better of it. Her decision. Do it now. Think later. Poppy got back into Lanky's area and noticed that her status said *married,* which was really sad and probably defensive too, to stop any men trying to chat her up online. But it was the other space she was interested in, the one at the top where people seemed to put that they were hungover and never going to drink again. It was the place where Lanky could leave a message for the world, or at least anyone who could check her out on Facebook.

Sorrel Golding's granddaughter Poppy would love to see her.

Well, that was the truth too. Poppy exited, shut down and joined Lanky for tea.

"I'll make a cake, shall I?" she asked.

"Oh, do!" said Lanky. "The scones all went. And the donkeys have got all the carrots."

Of course all of it was a kind of scrabbling around on the surface when things could have pulled Poppy under. It was what people did. Tea, cake, shopping, flower arranging, sweeping donkey muck. It filled most of the rest of the time between births and deaths, tribunals and police investigations, and people going missing for forty-six years. Or twenty-four hours. Was that all it was?

She spent most of the day with the donkeys, and most of that with Midge, who was very calm and almost completely out of her comfort zone, apart from her backside. Dan came and declared that he was happy with her and the Bach flowers were magic. But Freda was in an awkward mood and turned out to have worms, which meant checking every donkey, even though the six weeks since the last treatment weren't up, and Lanky kept muttering that she couldn't understand how it had happened. In the end it seemed that all the rest were clear, probably because many of them were wary of Freda and didn't go too near for fear of her evil eye.

Poppy did check Facebook but neither of her strategies had paid off. She tried calling Kane's phone but she had to leave a voicemail which probably sounded more emotional than she meant to be. Natalie popped in to check that they'd remembered the concert in Highover.

"Yes, of course," said Lanky, searching for something. "Eight o'clock, is it?"

"Seven fifteen," said Natalie, which sent Lanky into a muttering spin about stupid times and things that walked from cupboards and drawers. She said she wouldn't be ready and didn't these people realise that lives had to be lived. Poppy kept out of her way and took the red dress out of the wardrobe. Why not? It was her only night out of the whole stay.

She was thinking about ironing it when the mobile by the side of the bed vibrated. Kane! It was a one word message: *Call?*

Poppy fumbled and pressed and waited. It was ringing. Where was he?

"Hullo. Sorry …" he began.

"Where are you?"

"We've been staying somewhere my dad couldn't find us but it looks like it's sorted now. Jonathan's been genius. Is he really your godfather?"

"No." Suddenly she didn't know what to say. "Are you going back home, then?"

"Yeah. We're nearly there. Can I see you?"

"I'm going out."

Lanky was on the landing, eavesdropping shamelessly.

"Is that Kane?" she boomed. "He can have my ticket if he asks nicely."

Poppy grinned.

"Thank you!" she shouted.

"What ticket?" Kane was asking. "What's going on?"

"We're going to a concert," she said. "You'll come, won't you?"

Natalie drove and slotted in Bon Jovi, which made Poppy laugh out loud because it was *Living on a Prayer*. It gave her ideas, though, and she worded one carefully, realising that it was a bit like sending an email or a text and not being able to take it back to redraft. But *God bless Sorrel* was a good start.

They called for Kane, which involved Vic running in. Poppy knew he'd be checking that Karen and Al were all right. She guessed at police intervention, a court order or something. And some sort of second chance for Gary, whatever form that took, but lines laid down and rules that couldn't be bent. Natalie just sang along while they waited, but Poppy couldn't manage to join in. When Kane and Vic climbed in the back, Natalie stopped suddenly and asked Poppy to case up Bon Jovi and slot in Bach.

"Get used to it, Kane," she said, grinning back at him. "I have. And it's beautiful, if you go with it, stop fighting, breathe along."

He shrugged as if to say he might as well. Why not? Poppy would have liked to sit beside him, and tried not to keep turning round or finding him in the mirror. He sat quietly looking out of the window, and she wondered whether he was really trying to follow instructions or just thinking about something else. After a few minutes he looked back from the trees and houses and around at each of the others.

"'s good," he said. "I'd need something else to get me up in the morning."

"Cold wet flannel in the face works wonders," said Natalie.

Vic asked Kane about bands while Natalie chatted about the day and the donkeys, and Poppy pretended to be responding when really she was listening to the names Kane listed and trying to commit them to memory, even though she'd never heard of most of them. Soon Natalie smiled at her nods and hmmms as if she knew exactly what was going on. And then they arrived in Highover and parked opposite the big church, chosen as the venue, according to Vic, because it was moodier than the new arts centre.

"Lanky said her mum used to perform here," Natalie told Poppy, as they hurried in with an eye on the time, "as a mature woman but also as a child prodigy."

"Hebe?" asked Kane. "Cool!"

They exchanged smiles which Poppy saw Natalie notice, although Vic was busy returning waves.

Hebe in action. It was an idea Poppy hadn't considered. And it was supposed to be over, wasn't it? But why? Because she'd decided it should be? The church was large, high and cold, although brighter and less ugly inside than out. Vic called it a spiky, gloomy kind of Victorian baroque, in the same tone of voice he'd use for the phrase *reality TV*. Although it was still daylight outside, it took thousands of watts to combat the blackness, in spite of the gold trims. Poppy preferred the village's dumpy barn of a church. This was intimidating and flashy and miserable with it.

The pews were almost all full and the piano shone on its red carpet. Natalie and Vic both started conversations immediately, and were being acknowledged with smiles on all sides. Vic gestured to Poppy and Kane to get seats while there were still some spaces available. They found enough room for four just in time, leaving the two local celebs to disentangle themselves from their fans and squeeze in to join them at the last second. As the musicians who made up the quartet appeared to enthusiastic applause, Poppy realised that circumstances had allowed her to sit furthest to the side, next to Kane. Virtually unchaperoned! What would Miss Teale have to say about that!

Slipping off her cardigan, she felt so conspicuous in her dress that she might as well have been in her bikini. She remembered to cross her legs in a tuck-around way and wondered whether he'd noticed. Bows completed and clapping subsided, there followed a quick explanation about the love triangle that was Schumann, Clara Schumann and Brahms. Poppy knew most of it but it was like a favourite movie – there was more to savour each time.

As the music began Kane shifted to get comfortable. She gave him a smile. And as the emotion of the first piece began to tell, she glanced at him, hopeful but worried too, looking for reassurance that he was all right, that he wasn't bored, that he wasn't going to complain to his mates about the stuffy old stiffs in the audience or the chill in the churchy air. He didn't quite grin, not at once, but that was because he was in the middle of feeling something else, and she realised it was the music. She told herself to relax. Nothing could happen here in this crowd. It didn't work that way. The Hebe connection was information, that was all. Revelations over.

Just before the end he moved his arm as close to hers as it could hang without the two of them actually connecting like Ikea flat-packs. She felt his body heat, which hadn't all escaped yet, and imagined the fair hairs underneath the sleeve of his loose black shirt.

In the interval Natalie and Vic mingled over wine, but a frustrated and slightly panic-stricken Poppy had to queue for the toilet. Her period had started too soon and she had nothing with her at all. Hoping to last through the second half without too much embarrassment, Poppy emerged at last and looked for Kane. But even though she thought that identifying him in the crowd should be about as difficult as spotting a delphinium among daisies, she couldn't see him, not even in any of the corners.

He must be outside with the smokers, perhaps joining them, although she hoped not. She'd never smelt tobacco on him. Stepping out into the twilight she felt cold without her cardigan, which was on the pew. There was a small group in a smoky huddle but no Kane. She looked round the side.

No one there at all. At least, not at first. And then she knew that it wasn't over after all. The air was colder, the sound thinner, and the growl of engines not only scattered but at a different pitch. The church walls were just as dark and uninviting, and through the back of the stained glass the interior just as unknown. But in a slipped-back strip of time along the side of the building, Hebe Madison, no older than nine, held her mother's hand while her father Robert carried the case that hid her cello.

In paler light Hebe's skin was almost white, her cheekbones tightened. She was as black and cream as a photograph. A black velvet ribbon hung loose from her thick hair like apron strings, but the thick dress with soft, cream lace at the hem, cuffs and collar was almost bridal, except that it swayed full around long, black stockinged legs. Inside her free hand Poppy saw her fingers dig in against flesh. She looked up at Robert, who did not smile but gathered in his eyebrows, not so much questioning as demanding. He pushed open the door on a thick pile of voices, and ushered his wife and daughter ahead of him. Hebe the child prodigy was about to perform.

But would Poppy hear her? Only Poppy, set apart from the crowd, anchored within the present in a wreck of the past? Stepping forward to the opening door, Poppy felt the temperature change with the mood even before the image wavered and dispelled. A woman in a sequined top slipped through it, excusing herself to Poppy with a "Sorry, dear," and waved a man in. "Time!" she added when he did not follow. Poppy went through, looking around the church for Kane.

As she moved through the dispersing crowd filing back along pews, she felt a hand on her arm. Cool fingers spread through hers. For a moment she thought Kane had found her, but the skin was not his, neither rough nor bony. At her side she felt the other hand, loose and helpless, lifted up and encased between two palms. One finger tip found a wedding ring. The nearest person was a metre away, but still she felt the hands inside her own hands, and she knew them before she heard the voices, one young like hers, the other older but familiar. It was almost perfect unison.

Sorrel.

Poppy did not have to let them go. Tamarisk and Hebe passed on, away or through, and this time she felt it as clearly as if they had waved, the whole cast of ghosts, bowing and curtseying as if it was a curtain call. No more. Enough. It was finished now. Poppy stood alone in the high, chill building, watching the pattern of people murmuring contentedly into their rows like beads on a bright shiny abacus. The voices were lowering as they took their seats. But Kane was standing waving at her, as if she were stranded. She smiled and made her way across to sit beside him.

"Lost you," he muttered.

"I lost you," she said.

"You look great, by the way," he whispered as the musicians walked on to applause and a few cheers and whoops.

Poppy smiled. It was over now. It had to be.

As the violin wavered away an hour later into pure, dense silence awakened by the final note, Poppy felt tears on her face and blood trickling thin down one purple leg. Kane touched her hand and smiled, turning and pulling away as Vic asked him what he thought.

"Cool," he said. "Well ... hot."

Poppy, flushed and damp, and sure her face was as red as the blood, hurried away with a signal to Natalie. No wonder women used to call periods a curse. With no old-fashioned machines in the Ladies, not even the kind dispensing towels like mini nappies that made her walk like a cowboy, all she could do was wipe away the red stripe with toilet paper and spit, bundle up the tights in her handbag and return bare-legged. She needed to consult Natalie, but she was at the centre of a small crowd. Kane slid out towards her and they joined hands.

"Are you all right?"

She nodded.

"Too hot for tights?"

Of course some girls would have said they were *too hot for him or too hot to handle.* Poppy didn't think he expected any more than the faint *hmmmm* she gave him.

"Still on the quest?"

"I don't know. I don't think there's much more I can do."

"All the dragons slain then?"

She frowned.

"No way. I love dragons."

"Bet you haven't got a sword either."

She shook her head and he told her it looked a bit hopeless then.

"I've got a lot to tell you," she said.

"Good," said Kane. "Same."

Natalie and Vic appeared and Poppy wondered whether the sight of another couple holding hands and smiling might be alarming them. But they were the same as usual, except a little louder and more excitable. On the drive back they talked, back seat to front, all the way to Eddington, about the music, the performers and composers. The pastoral debriefing was brisk. According to Natalie, someone called Ellie Jarvis was looking really well after the op and Kevin Galloway was turning into a nice lad – although in her opinion a curtain of hair like that needed to be a) pulled and b) washed from time to time.

In all of seven minutes they were outside Kane's flat. Poppy made way for him to climb out. He thanked Vic and Natalie as she sat down again. Then he gave her a smile and said he'd see her tomorrow.

"It's my last day," she told him and he said he knew.

Vic started the engine and Poppy watched as Kane climbed the steps up to his door. He turned and waved, but it had a general sweep. It wasn't personal. She told herself not to watch because he wouldn't look back. And she didn't get the chance to prove it because Vic drove off and Natalie called back her concern.

"You okay, Poppy?"

Poppy explained about the period that wasn't due and Natalie said there were some tampons in their bathroom because her grown-up daughter had left some there. She'd run in and get them before they dropped Poppy back. Then Poppy closed her eyes and dozed until the car stopped again.

Vic pulled up on the vicarage drive, Natalie went to fetch the tampons and Poppy closed her eyes again. She opened them when Natalie came back almost at once. She wasn't carrying anything and she looked strange in the darkness, her eyes too bright. Vic got out of the car. She said there was someone there, by the back door. Vic told Poppy to wait, but she followed them a few steps behind. There was a dark shape, lumping there in the porch where they kept their bikes, mounding like a homeless man blanketed in a city doorway. Part of the shape moved and stood tall.

"Wait," said Vic to the others. "Hullo?" he called. "Can I help you?"

"I'm so sorry," said a woman's voice. "I didn't want to frighten anyone. I'm Sorrel Golding."

Chapter Twelve

Vic unlocked. He picked up a cello case and a holdall. As they all went inside, Sorrel smiled at Poppy and Poppy smiled back.

"Sorrel," said Natalie, unlike any other greeting Poppy had seen her give. "I must fetch your sister." She paused. "I need to warn her."

"Please," murmured Sorrel. "Please tell her I'm sorry." She reached out a hand to Poppy. "You wanted to see me. You're very like … the way I was."

"You haven't come after all this time just to look in the mirror!"

It came from Natalie, but it didn't sound like her. Poppy felt as if everything around her was changing and there was no way of following, keeping up and holding on. She stared at her grandmother. It was impossible not to stare, impossible to look away. Vic asked Sorrel to sit but she kept on standing, and Poppy took her in, soft top to pointed toes, as if she had to draw her after she'd faded away like the others, the ghosts. She took off her raincoat, which was a chaos of flowers, belted and chic. Underneath she wore an embroidered white shirt with a multicoloured string of glass beads at her throat, and black narrow jeans that tapered into red flats. Her thick hair was grey but glossy. Age had tamed it into smooth waves and held it sculpted. The pale grey-blue eyes she rested on Poppy had been doing a great deal of crying. But she seemed so utterly unlike a grandma, so elegant and scented, that she might have been an actress in a play, the lines in her skin etched in front of a mirror in a way that wasn't quite convincing.

Vic had put the kettle on and was asking about tea. Sorrel wanted black coffee. Poppy wanted to hold her and feel more, feel different. Sorrel looked around the immaculately clean and tidy kitchen and out of the window. She walked over to the roses in the vase on the window sill and breathed deeply.

"Poppy," she said quietly, "how is your father?"

Vic turned from the kettle. Poppy said he was all right.

"He's coming to pick me up tomorrow," she added.

"Ah," said Sorrel, "his mother's an old woman now."

She ignored a tear down the side of her nose until it caught the edge of her mouth. Then she wiped it like stray lipstick. Vic put down the mugs and asked her again to sit. This time she did, and leaned on her elbows, hands together. She blew on the coffee. Her mouth, which was glossed but not the bright colour of the old photos, was full but creased, the skin around tapering in like tiny pin tucks. Her hands were thin and veined, but the fingers were long and the nails cared for. She wore no rings.

"Do you play anything, Poppy?" she asked.

"Piano, mostly, but I did some cello and I'd like—"

The door opened and Lanky filled it, barefoot and wrapped loosely in her dressing gown, her face shiny with the cream she spread vigorously each night. Natalie was with her, but almost obliterated behind her.

"You can't do this, Sorrel!" she cried. "You have no right! I suppose because this is the vicarage we're supposed to call you the prodigal sister and kill a fatted calf, throw a party and praise the Lord because she who was lost is finally found and not dead after all …"

She stopped and her large hand covered her mouth, her fingers apart but shaking. Sorrel, having stood at the sight of her like a pupil for a schoolmistress, moved towards her, arms first. Poppy half-expected Lanky to shove her hard with another shout, louder this time. Instead her arms reached around her sister, whose head bent into her shoulder as their bodies closed together. Sorrel's hand stroked the skin down the back of Lanky's neck where the towelling colour ridged. There was sobbing, Lanky's loud enough to disturb the donkeys, Sorrel's lower and broken, requiring a handkerchief as she pulled away from her sister long enough to use it, then rested her head again.

Then Lanky separated herself to reach out a hand towards Poppy, pulling her in, one arm around her. Feeling their damp faces hot against her, and hearing them loud around her, Poppy cried too, until Lanky drew the embrace to a close and took a long, shaky breath. She leant against the fridge, wiping her face and chin with her hands. Vic signalled to Poppy and the three of them left the sisters alone in the kitchen, only to sit still and upright on the edges of the armchairs in the lounge as if they were expecting the Queen to arrive for tea. Suddenly Poppy stood, looking back to a small spot on the sofa.

"Sorry, Natalie! I need to change," said Poppy.

She had bled through her dress. Natalie took her up to the bathroom to show her the tampons in the cupboard, and said she'd come back to Lanky's with her and help her soak the stain out. She talked through the rescue operation, commentating as if radio listeners were relying on a progress report. Poppy was silent, and didn't want to feel helpless or unreal. She felt as if she'd witnessed some kind of accident and sooner or later someone was going to insist on an account, but for now she'd rather just keep standing.

It was late by the time Lanky's washing-up bowl was full of dress and Poppy was suddenly very tired.

"Sleep, Poppy," Natalie told her, "if you want to. I'll stay downstairs until they come back here."

Poppy lay down in the iron bed and closed her eyes. It had been a shock, but Sorrel was back and it was going to be all right now.

She woke, hot and whimpering, from a dream about Marty White, who tried to kiss her and fell down the stairs. She took in the room around her, the outlines vague in the landing light. Her door was ajar. She stared into the clock face. It was almost two in the morning, and she knew why she was awake.

The two female voices downstairs were modulated, responsive, cutting in and overlapping. They sounded comfortable, like friends in a café. Poppy padded downstairs and stood in the living room doorway. The sisters faced each other, one on each sofa. Lanky spread herself along one of them, a cushion propped up behind her head, while Sorrel sat

201

straight-backed and long-necked, one leg wrapped around the other and hands linked in her lap. Seeing Poppy, Lanky got up and hugged her.

"Sit here, Poppy," said Sorrel softly, persuasively, as if expecting her to refuse, and patted the space she'd made.

Poppy sat, and felt the closeness of her grandmother. It held her alert and ready, apprehensive and excited, as if her name would be called any moment to step up to the piano and play to a hall full of people.

"Your grandma has been telling me what she's been up to all this time," said Lanky, her eyes deep in the candlelight. Her voice sounded strange: controlled, flattened. "It's what they call a long story."

Poppy took that to mean she shouldn't ask for a rerun, not now anyway.

"I've been hearing about Derek," said Sorrel.

"Yes," said Lanky, and wiped her nose. "He held me together. Mortar Man."

Poppy hadn't heard her joke or sniffle about Derek before. Sorrel was looking sympathetic and Poppy realised she didn't know whether she'd ever married. And she'd missed the long story. She didn't even know who her grandfather was, or had been. It struck her that if Sorrel's status on Facebook said single, she'd be besieged by offers.

When she felt a hand touch her hair, she thought her grandmother must be smoothing it because it was wild from sleep, but she said it was fine, it was lovely.

"I'll make doorsteps," said Lanky. "I suppose you ladies want cucumber."

Sorrel opened her mouth at Poppy and they both smiled.

"Your grandmother's been a different kind of sister in France," added Lanky as she clambered off the sofa. "She's been a nun." She stopped in the doorway. "Ha!"

Her laugh started as a chuckle and rocked into something bigger in the kitchen. The next thing Poppy heard was "The Hills Are Alive With The Sound Of Music." She wondered whether this was what hysterical really meant: something to do with rage, trapped and rattling.

Turning away from it to Poppy, Sorrel explained that she'd been the kind of nun who doesn't just pray all day but works in the world.

"A kind of social work but with love more openly involved."

"God's love or yours?" asked Poppy.

"Both, I suppose."

"But you gave it up? Are you allowed to do that?"

Sorrel said it wasn't like prison! Poppy decided a five-year-old couldn't know less about holy orders than she did. She was sure the nuns must have told Sorrel that God forgave her, but Sorrel didn't look as if she'd ever believed it. What had changed since the photographs under the bed hadn't been about age. She'd got that well under control. What had passed away was the light.

Sorrel looked at the hands in her lap as if they were holding something she might break. Then she said she'd been sad to leave but had to, and Poppy didn't like to ask why.

"I hope no poor sap was in love with you!" called Lanky from the kitchen. It sounded like an accusation, over the soundtrack of a bread knife thudding and severing.

"I was busy trying to love all kinds of other people who needed help," said Sorrel quietly, as if confiding to Poppy, "which was much easier than loving myself."

"Enough touchy-feely for one night," Lanky shouted across the hall. "Stick to the bare bones."

"If I can think what they are," said Sorrel. "I ran an English café …"

"Like Tamarisk?" asked Poppy.

"Yes. Not even very far from hers. With scones. And I tried to forget who I was and be happy but nothing worked. And I got ill instead." She smoothed her shirt in her lap. "The kind of illness people are embarrassed to talk about. I was ill for a long time, on and off, but I'm getting better now."

Poppy had to think, but she got there. Sorrel meant the kind of illness people recovered from at Madison House.

"What about your singing?" she asked.

"I did sing, in the café, and played guitar. I did a little violin on the streets for a while, in Paris. I was never as talented as my mother."

"No one's going to contradict you!" yelled Lanky, which made Sorrel smile in a way that seemed to Poppy sadder than a scowl.

"I used to write songs with Steve," she remembered, smiling at Poppy on the beat of the name, and letting the pause that followed give it weight.

"Was that ..." she began, but didn't finish, because Sorrel nodded, eyes briefly closed. Such a young name, Poppy thought, for a grandfather.

"Silly mournful little things," continued Sorrel. "But I've been hearing music in my head since I've been better, and writing it down. Music for the cello, mostly. One day it might sound as good when I play it as it feels on the inside."

Lanky returned with the doorsteps, lumpy with cucumber chunks and spilling out rocket and watercress with the manners of a donkey. While they ate Poppy asked how Sorrel knew she wanted to see her, assuming somehow the Facebook message had done it, but it wasn't that. She had come to England the previous evening, and stayed at her Auntie Kath's. Lanky seemed cross that she'd got back in touch with Kath Golding, just a few miles away. Sorrel said Kath hadn't been at all surprised to see her, but then hadn't always seemed sure who she was, calling her Hebe once or twice.

"I had planned to come back twenty times," she said, a long way behind Lanky with her sandwiches and with less greenery in her lap. "But I had so many reasons not to. Guilt and shame and fear, of course ..."

"Of course," mocked Lanky emphatically, her mouth full.

"But also as time went by, an idea that everyone and everything would be healing and all I would do was rip things open again. And I knew my boy was safe. I knew he was being brought up with love. I told myself I wasn't the kind of mother he deserved."

"You never used to be so stupid," muttered Lanky, standing up and walking to the window. "Or such a coward."

Sorrel didn't cry or protest. She sat silently and Poppy gave her a look that was meant to explain that Lanky didn't mean it. But Lanky hadn't finished.

"You weren't the first teenage mother to dump a baby on the family because you weren't ready. Most of them usually grow up a bit and hope for understanding and a chance to try again. He would have loved you. He would have forgiven you in a blink!"

"It wasn't that." Sorrel shook her head and then lowered it. "I wanted my baby. I never thought of getting rid of it. Of him. But I couldn't come back. The police were looking for me ..."

"All this time and you still haven't knocked that nonsense into touch. It was a heart attack. They dropped the investigation. Whatever you did ..."

"I killed him."

Lanky turned to the window and glared at the darkness as if it filled her with contempt.

"Stop it."

"I believed it then and even now it still feels true."

Poppy tingled, legs clamp-tight. She felt like a spirit visiting a world where she didn't belong, out of place and understanding nothing. And then again like a child who shouldn't be up and would be sent to bed as soon as the adults remembered she existed.

Lanky walked back and sat down on the sofa facing them, catching the plate with her bad leg and scattering crumbs. Sorrel looked at them, the candlelight leaving them white on the chocolate brown carpet that Lanky said hid a multitude of sins.

"Don't you dare pick them up, Sorrel," she warned. "Just talk."

"I've never told it," said Sorrel, "not even to the nuns. And I've dreamed it so many times it's hard now to tell the difference. It's muddled and badly shot ..." She clasped her hands together tightly and rocked them backwards and forwards. Then she closed them together as if in prayer. "Not that I haven't practised it on the train until it didn't feel real ..."

Lanky lifted her chest as if she would hold her breath until her sister began. Sorrel placed her hands, spread, on her thighs.

"I left the club that night without my guitar because he was pestering me. I knew I'd have to get out of his orbit because he didn't understand NO."

"Marty slimeball White," spat Lanky.

"He was drunk even then. I slipped away after my spot and went to Steve's, thinking I was safe because I'd made sure Marty didn't know we were together. He made poor Deirdre tell him the address. So he turned up at Steve's place waving my guitar and saying if I wanted it back I'd have to be very nice to him. Steve told him I was carrying our child."

Sorrel looked away from both faces, eyes on the top of the bookcase with its worn-down candle slumping and flickering.

"So he started threatening and shoving, swearing and shouting and trying to grab me. He slapped my face. Steve tried to stop him. They were fighting. There was no phone in the place. Steve told me to run and get help. Of course Marty came after me then and the three of us were outside ... in the dark and the drizzle ... with Steve behind me and Marty grabbing at him, and he fell."

She stopped. The hands gripped, pulling the skirt into folds.

"Keep talking, Sorrel," Lanky told her. "Like a music exam. You don't stop playing however bad it gets."

"He lay still a moment, with a cut mouth ... red spittle trickling into a puddle ... but he was breathing. They were alcohol fumes. I picked up the guitar and we ran down the steps to the road."

"You left him alive," said Lanky, but Sorrel only looked back at her, mouth restless, and Poppy knew she hadn't finished.

"I went back," she said, "to check whether he was all right. He pulled at me. I was losing my balance and he was trying to twist my right arm behind me and pin me down. Steve was getting the Mini. I hit Marty with the guitar, left handed, but I shocked myself. *"Feeble,"* he jeered, *"like your singing."* But he stumbled and I ran. I kept expecting to hear him coming after me but it was quiet. He didn't even shout."

Her voice, which had gathered speed and risen, slowed and quietened again.

"As Steve drove off I couldn't look back. I kept asking whether he was moving, whether he was alive, and Steve said, *"He's fine."* He took me to my flat. I picked up some things. I said I was leaving and he looked away and said he'd go to his brother's for a while." She looked up at Lanky, one hand on her flat stomach. "That's when I knew he didn't love me, not enough, and I thought the baby inside me must have died because it felt like there was no air left to breathe."

The way Lanky turned her eyes to the ceiling then, Poppy almost heard her scoff like Ed, *Whoah, melodrama!* But when she spoke it was to mutter, as if she was addressing the skirting board.

"There's always air to breathe, Sorrel. The trick is to keep on doing it, no matter what."

Poppy looked away from Lanky and back to East London and the darkness, the steps and the blood in the saliva. It wasn't like the tribunal or the garden. She wasn't the audience watching the scene cut in like an advert interrupting the match. This time she could think herself through to the smell of things: rubbish in bins, a station toilet tang, and petrol in marbling puddles. More than anything she could feel the air locked inside Sorrel and how hard it was to keep on breathing.

Rain beat against Lanky's window, hard and sudden. No one mentioned it. Poppy wondered whether Sorrel had heard it and if she had, whether it was a different rain from another time.

"You telephoned for an ambulance," Poppy said, remembering the call from a female, "didn't you?"

"From a call box, first one I found that worked. I was going to come home, but I kept picturing the guitar hitting Marty. So I got the train to Dover and an early morning ferry to Calais, hitched south and took a cheap room. A day or two later I found an English paper in a café and read that he was dead. Suspicious circumstances. I didn't go near any more papers for weeks. I didn't dare try to contact Steve or Deirdre. I nearly went to the gendarmes, every day. And then I thought about my baby. I had to keep safe for him."

Poppy stood. It was horrible and unreal but it wasn't right.

"No!" she cried. "He fell down the steps. That's where they found the body. Either he had a heart attack which made him fall, or he fell and then his heart gave out. You didn't kill him." She looked from Sorrel to Lanky. "I saw it on the Internet."

"It's chicken and egg, my sweetheart," murmured Sorrel, almost like a song. "But you missed the important bit. The blow to the head. Without the blow, none of the rest would have happened ..."

"Cholesterol!" cried Lanky. "Booze, fags, drugs, fat, gangland stress! He had a heart attack. It wasn't your fault."

"It was all my fault." Sorrel's conviction was old and firm, rehearsed, established. "All of it."

Poppy realised it didn't matter what the autopsy said, or what verdict might have been declared by any jury. Sorrel had told herself she was an unfit mother. Her decision. Her certainty. And the fact that the case was finally closed, whenever the police had closed it, had made no difference at all. Something made Poppy think about Paul Golding and Hebe and the tribunal, about souls and darkness smothering.

"You had your baby," Poppy said. "Didn't you want to keep him?"

"Of course!" Sorrel looked so shocked Poppy wished it back. "It wasn't just that every day I woke expecting to be found, arrested, and brought back to England to be tried for murder. It was how I felt about myself, and the kind of mother I'd be."

"Even if that sorry smack you gave him made any kind of difference," said Lanky, "and I know you, Sorrel, I know a teddy would hit harder with its little velvet paw – it was self-defence. Even if it got to court, any barrister …"

"But the press would lap it up. Murder and the pacifist's daughter. A gift! They'd paint me as a slut, and have their own ideas whose baby I was carrying. I couldn't name Steve. My little boy would have been born into a news story with a notorious mother."

Lanky slapped her hands to her head as if she couldn't listen or think any more.

"So, Poppy, to cut a long story short, arrangements were made. Hebe and Paul had to go to France and meet an old friend of Tamarisk's, who handed the baby over."

"They sent me the cello," said Sorrel.

"Gifts all round! Good as Christmas!" Lanky cried. "Of course if the police had still seriously suspected Sorrel by then, the game would, as they say, have been up."

"I often thought," said Sorrel slowly, as if she was remembering carefully, and respecting the truth, "that I'd wait until I was sure it was over, and come back for him."

"I know just what you mean," said Lanky. "I often think about turfing all the crud out of my kitchen cupboards, but I never do it. I never even convince myself I might."

She flung her arms out towards the doorway as if to direct anyone who wished to check for evidence. "You never came," she said, "not even …"

Not even when Paul died, thought Poppy, picturing the funerals Sorrel never attended. Looking across she realised Sorrel was thinking about them too.

211

"Kath got word to me when Father died," she told Poppy. "I became ill. I'd changed my name by then and moved south. I gave the hospital lies; I almost believed them. I didn't know about my mother's death, not for years. Kath was in New Zealand by then and nobody here knew where I was ..."

"So I took your son. Of course I did! But don't go thinking you were some kind of Lady Bountiful bestowing on me the gift of life," said Lanky. "I grew to love him. I wasn't a natural mother like you would have been. Too prickly and odd even then."

Sorrel's mouth opened, but Lanky didn't pause long enough to be thanked – although Poppy saw the word shaped, silently and unfinished.

"I did my best, I hope, and Derek made up for my deficiencies. We made the best of what you'd done, that's all. Your David wanted you. He's always wanted you. Everyone always did."

Next to her on the sofa Sorrel sat still and fine but shaking inside.

"Please, Lanky," murmured Poppy, and she knelt down on the crumbs and the chocolate carpet and reached around Lanky's legs. Her great aunt leaned down and closed her own arms around her. She wasn't wailing this time. It was all inside.

When they pulled apart Sorrel had gone. They rushed to the door where she had picked up her holdall and was reaching for the cello case standing like an Egyptian sarcophagus against the wall.

"I'm so sorry," she said.

Lanky grabbed the bag and dropped it with a clunk against the wall.

"You're not going anywhere!"

Her face was shadowed as she blocked the way. The only light came from the lounge and the thin moon opaque through the frosted panel in the door. She turned the key in the lock.

"So you can't sneak off in the night and leave a note. Not this time." She took Sorrel's hands in hers only to let them go. "It's no good having grace and manners if you don't know how to be forgiven."

"My mum says no one should ever be judged," said Poppy, "by the worst thing they've ever done."

For a moment she thought Lanky was going to laugh like Ed did, when she said something important and serious as if it was a line in the climax to a film. She didn't. She just told Sorrel that she'd meet Poppy's mother tomorrow.

"David's wife. Your daughter-in-law, in case you're not keeping up."

"I know who she is," murmured Sorrel. "She must be a good woman."

"She's had to be. And she'll love you, of course. We'll be one big happy family." Lanky snorted. "But we need some sleep or I might be even more badly behaved tomorrow."

Poppy stared. She lifted one hand. It was trying to read the time on Derek's old watch around Lanky's wrist that reminded her.

"Sorrel," she said, "you didn't take Marty's watch. He was robbed after you'd gone. Whoever took it must have hit him or kicked him. A blow to the head."

She explained: the newspaper extracts on the net, before Lanky had interrupted. And a sentence on screen that she'd never finished until now. The two of them looked at Sorrel but she didn't move. She couldn't seem to receive or absorb or believe.

But Lanky could. She'd stopped paying any attention, she said. She'd had enough, more than enough. She'd never heard, never read …

Her shoulders fell and her hands agitated around her face and mouth, pressing, meeting, and then extended, palms up, towards her sister. Poppy watched and waited. Sorrel clasped Lanky's hands in the space between them and thanked her again and again, but Lanky turned her head away like a child who wouldn't listen.

"I'm angry," muttered Lanky, her teeth fierce. "I'm angry because you stole from us. You took from us what we loved more than anything. We had to do without you. It was too much to lose. For David especially. And for me too."

Poppy could see Sorrel didn't know what to say. They were both spent. It felt as if the last crackle in the air had loosened to a hiss and died.

"We don't have to do without her any more," she said.

Less than four hours later Poppy stirred on the sofa where she'd slept so Sorrel could have her bed, and joined the two women for breakfast, a quiet one. Then they went out to see the donkeys.

Everything was quite normal at first: buckets kicked, bottoms rubbed, heads nuzzling, ears presented to be scratched, and teeth bared in affection by the attention-seekers, the usual suspects, while the rest hung back doing whatever it was they were busy doing without moving much of a muscle. Sorrel, swamped in one of Lanky's sweatshirts against a crisp morning breeze, seemed overwhelmed in a pleased sort of way and talked softly in the centre of the crowd. Lanky moved around, chirpy and playful, making an effort, Poppy thought, to be her normal self, in case they sensed something.

"Is George …?" began Sorrel.

"Hanging on," said Lanky, pointing.

Sorrel started walking. Poppy looked away, distracted by a demanding Freda. She heard the hooves' pace before she saw. George was on the move and even the other donkeys stirred away in surprise. Poppy remembered. The schoolgirl sisters and Mac Trandle's donkey that shouldn't have been alone. George remembered too. Braying, he nudged his muzzle into Sorrel's chest, and kept turning and stroking his head against her until he just let it hang low and still for her to pat and scruffle.

"Very Hollywood," said Lanky, and started to explain about feeding.

Poppy found a moment to ask her quietly later on about her dad and what he knew, because she thought someone needed to prepare him before he arrived to find his mother at the door. Lanky said Vic was probably on the phone as they spoke. Poppy couldn't imagine what her dad would say or do. What he'd feel was even harder to sort and name.

"Kane's coming later, Poppy," Lanky told her. "He's got his own stuff going on and so have we. But he'll be here."

"Okay," said Poppy, trying not to ask when.

Maybe it was the way Lanky arranged it. Kane cycled in on a new bike minutes before Poppy's parents arrived, so that they'd only had time to exchange smiles and the most important information. In Kane's case it involved the news that his old headmaster had said he was welcome back at the start of term, and in Poppy's meant introducing her grandmother.

Then she pointed out her dad, as he emerged slowly from the passenger seat. But another introduction came first and Lanky did that one, hugging him quickly, whispering something. Her father hung back, looking and not moving, his mouth not holding its line. It was Anna Beth who kissed both Sorrel's cheeks, and Sorrel kissed back, then stepped aside to stand in front of him, close enough for him to reach out when he wanted to, if he wanted to. She only waited a moment. Then she held his shoulders and laid her cheeks against his, and his head sank as he let her hold him. They walked into the house without speaking and no one followed.

Poppy's mum slipped her arm in hers.

"I've no idea what you've been doing here. And if I'd had as much as an inkling of any of this ten days ago I'd have chained you to your room ..." She sighed. "He never thought he'd see her again."

"Poppy has to say goodbye to Kane," announced Lanky, picking straw from her hair, "so I suggest we leave them to it and have a cup of tea at the vicarage," and Poppy could only blush and be grateful she didn't wink as she took her mother away.

Kane asked Poppy if she wanted to go to see Midge and Ben.

"Sure," she said, "in a bit."

They sat in the caravan, leaving the door open so no one would get any ideas. Joss was on the padded seat along with a lot of papers and cushions and a dream catcher that had fallen down and was waiting to be hung again. The cat accepted the opportunity offered by Poppy's lap, and permitted stroking. Kane found a new position for the dream catcher so that the light broke through it. When he sat down next to Poppy, Joss sprang down and out into the stable yard.

"It's 'cos I call her moggy, and tell her to scram," he said. "Cats kill things."

"They can't help it."

"I prefer donkeys."

It was quite snug in the caravan, and no more of a mess than the office upstairs. Amongst the clutter they spotted an old biscuit tin with a dented lid, which they managed to open after a lot of pulling and overacting.

Poppy glanced across to the house and Kane must have known she was wondering. She told him the word reunion didn't quite seem to cover it.

"Mission accomplished then," said Kane. "You should set up a business: No quest too large."

She started to tell him everything, Marty White and Steve and France … but then she stopped.

"Kane," she said, "do you mind if I write it down, in a letter?"

He grinned.

"I never get letters. Well, only official ones. I'm not planning on getting any more of those."

"Good," she said.

"Yeah, I'd like a letter. I bet you write really neatly, with everything at the same angle, all round and curvy."

"Yes!"

"If you send me Sorrel's story I'll tell you about smashing the estate agent's window because we had our house repossessed." He pulled a face that suggested the absence of his brain at the time. "And the windscreen of a four-by-four belonging to a debt collector, but he's inside now. I'm not angry any more. Not often, anyway. It's not a condition."

She wasn't surprised, just sorry. He told her there was no need to say anything so she didn't.

"Displacement," he added, "obviously. Or was it transference? I'm rusty. I wanted to hit my dad but I don't do people. That's his speciality."

There was one biscuit left in the tin now so they shared it, alternate bites. He accused her of leaving it soggy at the edges so she snatched the last bit and placed it in her mouth with yum yum eyes.

"Oy!" he said. "You know I said I'm not angry any more …"

She laughed and he leaned in. She thought he was going to push her off the seat but he kissed her on the cheek where it bulged with biscuit. She swallowed and smiled.

"Do you think any mum is better than none?" she asked.

"Sorrel Golding is better than none," he said.

"How can you tell?"

"I'm a good judge of character." He grinned. "I knew you were a nutter right off." He looked out to the field. "She's a flower girl, you can tell that. Looks just like you."

Poppy smiled. She got up and he followed, close by her side, almost touching, arms in a rhythm as they walked up onto the field.

Ben was grazing half-heartedly and Midge was watching him, back hooves in her corner. Kane walked casually over and placed his hand down on her neck in one smooth, light and very slow movement.

"Hey, gorgeous," he said, lining up eye contact as best he could. "Come out to play."

Poppy gave Midge her most encouraging look, full of faith. Midge looked back. Kane leaned his head down towards hers and blew warm air on her mane. He turned his mouth and spoke into her ear, stroking with his right hand and keeping his left firm and soft on her neck. Then he pulled slowly away.

He stepped gradually backwards, one pace, two. He stopped.

"Now, Midge," he said, and held out a hand, fingers curling to beckon, and Midge stepped across the grass to meet him. One hoof after another. Unled and willing, purposeful and light. A sequence of steps that left the corner behind. Ben made a thin snuffle through his nose and lifted his head. The two of them moved across to lean in, nose to nose.

Kane grinned at her, hands out on both sides, clownish and *Wouldjabelieve it?* Poppy's smile felt wide as a police searchlight. She wanted to hug them both, like she'd done with Lanky and Sorrel in the kitchen. Instead she just stood still and watched the donkeys settle. A step too far. Things took time. Words like healing and forgiving had been knocking around in her head like notes of a tune that wasn't written yet.

"You're not the only one who can work wonders," he told her, quietly, as if he couldn't be completely sure that a full-throttle cocky whoop wouldn't erase the miracle and get Midge kicking off again. "Still," he said, "my dad was right about you. You're way too good for me."

"I don't know," she said, giving him a look that she hoped was cheekier than coy. "You might be underrated."

"Also too young."

She shrugged.

"I'll get older. It happens when you just keep on breathing."

"You're full of yourself today, aren't you?"

She did a nodding dog admission. It would have been hard to say what she was full of, but there was plenty of it. The house felt close and she tried to imagine her dad inside it with Sorrel. He didn't have that rage and savage black humour that Lanky wielded around her like a sword in case anyone thought she was soft. But Poppy knew now that he'd never had Sorrel's light to lose.

"Listen," said Kane. "What's that?"

Poppy heard a window jerk open in the living room. And another. Her father was there briefly in each of them, arms leaning to push them outwards. She didn't think he saw her but maybe he wasn't looking. Out through the space a cello cried, like a widow in one of those countries where it was okay to moan and howl in the street. It wasn't any music she'd heard before and didn't seem to belong to any time. Smiling, she realised it was like her T-shirt, her favourite one. Wild and free. It was different and strange and what Ed would call *weird* but she liked it. Faint, it flickered and gutted, hung like a hope that melted in rain. Then it gathered itself up and thickened with sunshine till it was gold as an altar piece from an old millennium, and whiter than peace doves lifting on a banner.

"Turn it up!" shouted Kane. He smiled at Poppy. "Let's get those donkeys dancing."

She was leaving soon and she didn't know why she felt so happy when she should be crying like the cello. They stood listening, still as Midge and Ben.

"It's music to breathe to," she told him.

"Yes, Poppy," he said, eyebrows lifting with his voice.

"And you haven't been around donkeys long enough to know this, Kane," she said, with lashings of primmest patience, "so your ignorance is excusable, but I'm afraid they never dance."

"Never?"

She smiled, shook her head and took a few steps closer to the music. Following, he pulled her to a stop, grabbed her arms and lifted them at the elbows, placing her hands on his shoulders while his own rested on her waist.

"I do," he said. "Tap and ballroom. Age nine. Says Merit on the certificate."

Poppy edged her feet around, feeling like poor blind Cinnabar and glad there was no bucket to kick as another assumption fell to the dirt. But as her cheeks burned and she held her head too low a few inches from his, the cello rose. It tapered trembling, high as a hawk on air, shining like a raindrop under sun, and stopped. They stood listening a moment, waiting, but it was finished.

Kane let go of her hands. He smiled, and she thought he looked embarrassed, but disappointed too.

"Shame," he said. "I can see you've got a lot to learn."

"That's all right," said Poppy. "There's time."